HEARTS AFIRE

HEARTS AFIRE

SHAMEKA S ERBY

Contents

Dedicated to everyone who loves love, and the day of love

May love find me, and all of us

Author's Note

The stories in this work are short stories ~12,000 words each, and the central theme is Valentine's Day. They will be somewhat fast-paced and the romance will either develop quickly, or the couple will be established when the story begins. This is an open door romance--there are explicit sex scenes on page.

Although I have done my best to make them stand alone, it is still my belief you will have a MUCH more enjoyable experience if you read All I Want for Christmas is Two before reading this. Thank you for giving my work a chance and please make the best decision for you.

Content warnings for each individual story are on the title pages.

Staying Power

Nate Harper is a talented barber, and the one younger, single, man in Luna Lake that Sassy Dumont can't have. He does want her; he just doesn't want to be seen as a throwaway lover. But after a nasty divorce, Syreeta Dumont is happy with her freedom and refuses to trust any man with her heart again. Can Nate change her mind?

Content Warning: Mentions of past marital abuse, and use of derogatory language toward the FMC (NOT by the MMC)

An Undeniable Pull

October 19th, 2024
Nathan "Nate" Harper

"The big 4-0! How does it feel, my nigga?" Hassan asked Nate as they sat at *Bottoms Up*, the most popular bar in Luna Lake. The two of them worked side-by-side all day at *Luna Cutz*, the barbershop Hassan took over from his grandfather, and then Hassan offered to buy drinks when he remembered it was Nate's birthday.

"It feels pretty much the same. I'm just happy to be here, you know?" Nate Harper replied. Hassan nodded, as if he understood. The two of them were at a table at the back, watching the guys around them argue over a pool game.

Bottoms Up was as old as the barbershop, and was one of many businesses owned by Titus Hobbs. The bar was managed by his son Elias, and his daughter-in-law Evangeline, or Vangie, as everyone called her. Although there were other places to hang out, including *Luna Puffs*, the local cigar bar, and *Melodies*, a brand-new lounge/ jazz club, the best friends preferred the laid-back environment of the bar. They loved playing pool, or darts, or shooting the shit in a place where they could still wear the clothes they'd worn to work.

"You gonna do anything special? Take a vacation, go to the casino, anything?" Hassan pressed. Nate chuckled, shaking his head.

"I want some peace for my birthday, man. A vacation sounds good, but if I'm gonna be on a beach, I want a nice pair of soft titties to rest my head on, if you catch my meaning."

"I do. But you can still go. Maybe you'll meet someone there, you never know."

"Nah, Hass. I don't want to be on no fly-by-night shit. A vacation fling is not even where my head is right now. I want a woman of my own, a woman I can be with," Nate said. Hassan nodded. He'd been married to Everly for the last nineteen years, so Nate knew he understood how a good woman could enhance your happiness. Hassan and Ever were made for each other, and Nate couldn't help but be envious of their love.

"I got you, Nate. And I'm not surprised. You haven't dated anyone since you and Sabrina Harlem tried to get something going last year, right?" Hassan said.

Nate snorted. "I barely even count that, to be honest. Bri is a beautiful woman, but she's only 32 and still trying to establish herself as a person. She barely even knows what she wants to get out of a relationship. According to her, I'm too 'old-acting' and I need to loosen up. Meanwhile, I never knew if she liked me for me, or if she simply wanted to have a man because Kira has one now," Nate said back. Hassan laughed, but he didn't refute the statement.

He and Sabrina Harlem were hooked up by her twin sister and his coworker, Shakira. They dated for a couple of months, but it fell flat. Nate needed someone who knew her place in the world already, and didn't need nudging into expressing their expectations. Sabrina was new on the Luna Lake police force when they started dating, trying to make her presence known and get her voice heard in a literal boys' club, and it was rough at first. She brought a lot of it home with her, and it affected them. Nate understood her struggle, but he wasn't obligated to bear the brunt of her growing pains from her job. Sabrina seemed to be in a good place now, and paired with Rick Wilkins as her partner, so she was settling down some, but Nate didn't go backwards. There was no reason for him to think it would work this time.

"Whether you count it or not, it's been a long ass time, man. Get back out there. Matter fact, it's your birthday. Why don't you go speak to one of those pretty women at the bar? Flex your muscles, see if you still got it."

Nate laughed. "Naw man. You can tell you been out the game, Hass. You don't even sound right stringing those words together. Besides, I already know who I want. I just don't think I'm gonna get her."

"Wait, you already set your sights on somebody? How did I miss it? Who is she?"

As soon as Hassan finished talking, the bar door opened, and she walked in. Nate sat up straight in his chair, his throat suddenly dry. She was giggling at something her companion was saying and her laughter floated through the bar, over the music, and into his ears like a melody meant only for him. Nate sighed. She was still the most beautiful woman he'd ever seen in his life.

Hassan noticed his attention had drifted. "Yo, Nate. Where'd you go? Who are you—"

"I'll be right back," Nate interrupted him and stood up. He made his way to the bar, his focus still on her and her date. When he was closer, she looked up, their gazes clashing. The two of them stared, both filled with heat and hunger. Nate wanted her. He knew she felt it too. But he refused to be one of her boy toys. He refused to share her, to hide her, or to accept a temporary relationship. He wanted Syreeta "Sassy" Dumont all to himself, and he wanted her forever. For those reasons, he'd probably never have her.

"Let me get two more whiskeys and two more beers," Nate said to the bartender, still sneaking glances at Syreeta at the end of the bar. She was wearing a pink, low-cut top and her jeans looked painted on. Her golden-brown skin seemed smooth and soft where her breasts were pushing out of her shirt, and Nate wanted to kiss her there. Syreeta was a full-bodied woman, packing plenty of breasts, hips, thighs, and ass. But she also had some chub in her belly and arms and cheeks and those were Nate's favorite parts of her. All that body, combined with hair to her elbows and the most adorable cat-eyeglasses, Syreeta Dumont was a "bad bitch," as the kids say, and she knew it.

Tonight, she was with Sharif Sims, some lame ass wannabe who played at being a barber because his cousin owned a *Sharp Shears* franchise. *Sharp Shears* was a national barbershop chain, with no authenticity or genuine style; it was the fast food of barbershops. But they were cheap, fast, and "good enough," so the Luna Lake location was Hassan's biggest competition.

The bartender worked quickly and soon Nate had two cold bottles of beer and two rocks glasses on a tray. He stole one last look at Syreeta and her date and then turned away. It clearly wasn't meant to be. *Then why can't you get her out of your fucking head, Nathan,* he berated himself. He sighed and shook his head. He was forty years old, which meant he was too damn old to chase after a woman who didn't want him. He balanced the tray and left the bar.

"Happy birthday, Nathan," floated in the air behind him, and he turned back again. Syreeta gave him a small smile, and a wave.

"Thanks," he returned and finally rejoined Hassan. Someone had taken away their empty beers and glasses, so Nate sat the entire tray down, before retaking his seat.

"Damn, you got it bad," Hassan mumbled, grabbing a beer and taking a long drink. Nate stared at his friend. Was he really so obvious?

"What you talking about?" he asked, trying to play it off. Hassan laughed out loud.

"Nigga, don't even try it. I could feel the heat between you and Sassy from over here. What's up with you and her? She shoot you down?"

"Naw, I shot *her* down," Nate admitted.

Hassan froze, his rocks glass halfway to his mouth. "You serious? How come?"

Nate sighed. "Because I can see myself taking all my vacations with her. I can see us laid up forever. I want Syreeta bad, man. I think she's the woman I can go the distance with. But all she wanna do is play. I don't want to be one of her options. I'm the best nigga for her, and I deserve to be her only nigga. She want me to be okay with being temporary, and I'm not. I told her ain't nothing happening until she get her mind right."

"Damn, Nate. Look at you, knowing your worth and shit. I'm proud of you, my nigga. And I understand where you coming from, but Sassy's been through a lot, man. From what I hear, her ex really did a number on her, not only during the marriage, but during the divorce too. He tried to make sure she walked away with nothing, and it was a long process for her to finally get what she deserved. I understand her hesitance," Hassan offered.

"I understand it too. I told her we could go slow, and that I'd do whatever it took to earn her trust. I don't have a problem working for her. But she won't even give us a chance. She wants me to accept less than I need, and what I know we both deserve. I won't, Hass. I'm too old for games."

"I get it, and I agree. Maybe it ain't meant to be, or at least not meant to be right now. Sorry, man. For what it's worth, I think y'all would be good together," Hassan said.

"I know we would. Hopefully one day she knows it too," Nate said back. He sipped his beer, and stared over at Syreeta, not even caring if people saw him so focused on her when she was with someone else. In Nate's mind, she was his, anyway. Plus, she remembered his birthday. It didn't sound like much, but to him it was progress.

<u>December 23rd, 2024</u>
<u>Sassy</u>

Syreeta "Sassy" Dumont left the diner and headed to her car. Antonio Hobbs was fine as hell, but not for her. Flirting with him was mere muscle memory; she wasn't in the mood to date anyone right now, anyway. She started her car, letting it warm a little. Sassy was hoping to get a good parking spot behind the library and then walk up Main Street to the parade. Luna Lake's Christmas Parade was a lively affair, with fun, food, and floats of all kinds—there was even booze if you stayed until the end. Maddy's Ice Cream Shop was usually the last float in the parade, and she handed out cookie dough bites to the kids, and root beer floats made with hard root beer to the adults. It was rumored she even added some of Mr. Titus's famous homemade moonshine. The free treats started as an incentive to get people to stay until the end of the parade instead of walking off after the popular floats passed. It was working, and Sassy could hardly wait to taste hers.

The drive to the library was short, and Sassy was able to get the parking space she wanted. She hopped out quickly and walked around to the front, heading up the block to where everyone was starting to gather. She threw up a wave to Ms. Minnie, who was in her booth, surrounded by her Snack Packs, little lunchboxes with nibbles of food for people to enjoy as they watched the parade. They were selling fast, like they did every year, and Sassy smiled at Ms. Minnie's bravery. She wasn't afraid to try new things, put herself out there. She was a good businesswoman, and Sassy was sure the diner wouldn't be thriving like it was if her no-good baby daddy had stuck around instead of leaving her and her daughter Paige. Men tended to ruin good things, which was why Sassy didn't bother with them anymore past dick and laughs.

Her cellphone buzzed, and she pulled it from her coat pocket, frowning as she looked at the screen. And here was a man on her phone, proving her point. They even knew how to ruin a damn goodbye.

"Yes, Sharif?" she said pleasantly.

"Sup, Sass. Why I ain't heard from you?" Sharif Sims said back, his voice going whiny like he was pouting. Sassy sighed. It was so tiring when they acted like they didn't get it.

"You're not supposed to hear from me, love. We agreed to move on, remember?"

"Yeah, but I ain't seen you with nobody. Assumed you hadn't replaced me yet because you miss a nigga," Sharif went on. Sassy rolled her eyes.

"You know what happens when you assume, Sharif. Look, we had a good time. But you know I don't stay still for too long. You said you were okay with it."

"I am okay with it. You ain't gotta marry a nigga; I just want to fall through sometimes, you know? Get a little piece and go about my business. I wasn't trying to bother you."

Then why are you on my phone, Sassy thought. She sat the phone on the low wall she was leaning against and put him on speaker so she could look for her damn earpods.

"I explained my requirements to you. We do what we do, while it feels good. I walk away clean, and I don't backslide. You said you understood, and you agreed," Sassy explained, getting annoyed. She was standing on the street in the cold, while all the good parade watching spots were filling up because men ruined everything. Every. Damn. Thing. Sharif didn't even want her for real, and he was still ruining this break-up.

"I know what we agreed, but you ain't bout to play me like no little ass boy, Sass. I doubt anybody else is hitting it like I was, cause I ain't seen you wit nobody. You know you been missing me," Sharif stated confidently. Sassy wanted to laugh, but she refrained. Men could be violent when you threatened their egos. It was a lesson she'd learned the hard way.

"Sharif, I don't want to do this, okay? I like you, but I can't be what you want."

"Why? You got some other nigga?"

"I—"

"Yes, she does, and I do my job well. Now, we have a date to watch the parade. Goodbye," Nathan Harper spoke into her phone and then hung it up, winking at her. Sassy was speechless, and suddenly hot. She hadn't even heard him approach, but here he was, getting into her business, messing with her, *claiming* her. She convinced herself he'd taken all his relationship demands to some other woman and forgotten all about her. But he was right here, in her space, making her breathe hard and sweat inside her coat. Sassy wanted to be humiliated—how much of her conversation had he heard? But he smelled so good, and he was smiling with his perfect white teeth and all she could register in her brain was Nathan Harper telling someone he was her new man, and he did his job well. When in the world did he get so arrogant, and why did she like it so much?

It was an undeniable fact Nathan Harper was a walking, talking, rose session inspiration with his sable skin and topaz-colored eyes. The gold tones sparkled in the sun, and it was a joy to have his gaze on you. His body was muscled—he was a big boy, and tall, nearly towering over her five-foot-seven at six-foot-three. He was a star barber, careful and meticulous with his hands, but didn't have any hair himself, and Sassy found herself wanting to kiss his smooth, bald, head while he held her tight. The lack of hair didn't extend to his face; he was fully bearded, and all she could think about when she saw the pillow of bushy softness surrounding his lips was sitting on it.

"Nathan, what are you doing?" she said, trying to get her voice and body under control.

He smirked. "Sounds like I was saving you, Syreeta. You're welcome. Now come on, the parade's about to start." He held out his arm, expecting her to take it, and her brain couldn't get the "hell no" message to her body fast enough because she did. Moments later, they were walking up Main Street, and Sassy was trying to figure out how it happened. They passed people they both knew, and no one even batted an eye at seeing them together. Then she realized everyone probably assumed Nathan was her new temporary lover. The thought made her a little sad. She wouldn't mind being with someone like Nathan, but he wanted a commitment from her, a real relationship, and she didn't do those anymore. Nathan refused to be one of her discarded lovers, and while she understood and even admired his stance, she couldn't help feeling like she was missing something not letting him into her life.

He stopped them in front of *The Neverending TBR*, Luna Lake's bookstore, where there were two chairs right at the curb.

"Lilah saved me the good seats in front of her store. Come on," Nathan said, guiding her into a seat and then sitting next to her.

Sassy wanted to pout. Why would he interrupt her phone call if he was supposed to be with someone else?

"So... I'm in Lilah's seat?" she asked, not even hiding the bite in her voice.

Nathan chuckled. "Are you jealous, Syreeta Dumont?" he teased. He stroked her cheek.

Sassy slapped his hand away. "Of course not. W-why would I be—I was—I only—"

"You're so flustered you can't even talk," he whispered, sliding his arm around her waist, "My poor baby. You are jealous, and as much as I want to drag this out and have some fun with you, I won't. Lilah and I are friends, Syreeta. We're not involved, and we've never been involved."

"I—I mean, I don't care if you are. I don't have the right—"

"You have every right, baby love. Cause you know who I belong to, same as I do. It's why I'm reassuring you. I was saving these seats for my parents, but they wanted to sit with my dad's fishing buddies. When I saw you headed this way, I decided I would ask you to sit with me. When you stopped, I thought something was wrong, so I went to make sure you were good," Nathan finished, looking right into her eyes. He was telling the truth, and admitting he belonged to her and Sassy was swooning. She was 49 years old, for goodness' sake. Nathan was nearly a decade her junior; he wasn't supposed to have her all out of sorts, and... breathless. Christ on a cracker, she was breathless over a man! This was not good.

"Nathan... I can't give you what you want," she said lowly, sighing at the end. She needed to cut him down now, get him out of her system. Maybe if she hurt his feelings enough, he'd stop wishing for things that weren't going to happen... and she'd stop wishing for them too. Nate tightened his arms around her waist.

"Can't or are afraid to?" he questioned in her ear, his breath warm. Sassy turned, her lips pursed to retort, but he kissed them, sending a zing of electricity through her body and effectively silencing her.

"We can talk about it later. The parade's starting." He closed the conversation and directed her attention to the majorette and dance troupe, dressed in red velvet costumes with antler headbands, leading the way for the band behind them. Sassy heard the strained horns and offbeat drums of the Luna Lake High Marching Band and briefly hoped her taxes this year would go toward a worthy cause, like hiring a new band director. But all of it was background noise to the fireworks going on in her body. Nathan Harper kissed her! Sweetly, but so casually, like they shared kisses all the time, like he was used to it, like he was *supposed* to be kissing her. This was not good.

By the time Maddy's Ice Cream Shop float made its way down the street, Sassy needed something to cool down in the worst way. For the entire parade, Nathan held her, whispered funny comments in her ear, kissed her cheek and stared into her eyes, like he couldn't believe he was there with her. She was a puddle of lust and confusion now, and nearly on the verge of begging him to come home with her. The only thing to disrupt their bubble was a fight on the other side of the street, but once they said it was Jerome Hobbs, she and Nathan went back to their own world. Jerome was an asshole, and Sassy was sure whatever he got, he deserved.

Everyone stepped into the street and Maddy and her workers passed out clear, lidded to-go cups full of root beer float and straws to go with them. When Lilah came out of the bookstore to get hers, Nate gestured to the two chairs they'd been sitting in.

"Appreciate you, LJ. You can take the chairs. Syreeta and I are gonna stroll Main Street for a while before I walk her to her car."

He offered his arm again and Sassy took it, as Lilah smiled and winked at them. She waved and Nathan nodded, and then they were walking.

"LJ?" she wondered aloud. Nathan laughed.

"Her full name is Lilah Jean," he explained, "I've been calling her LJ since Hass introduced us. They used to hang together a lot because they were the same age. When we were all ten years old, Hass wanted his favorite cousin, to meet his best friend. The three of us have been tight ever since."

"Sometimes I forget how long most people here have known each other. It must be nice having so much history," she said, pushing down her sad feelings. She unwrapped her straw and put it in her float, taking a sip. The sweet, creamy ice cream, the fizz of the root beer, and the subtle kick mixed on her tongue and Sassy felt better.

Nate stopped them in front of Everly Hobbs-Meadows' flower shop, *Luna in Bloom*. The front window was filled with poinsettias and paperwhites and accented with amaryllis. There were twinkly lights framing the space and a "Happy Holidays" sign hanging over the display.

"You don't have to hide that you've had a hard time, Syreeta," Nathan spoke quietly, as if he was afraid to scare her, "I know something hurtful brought you here, and I know your past wasn't like mine. But you don't have to be embarrassed about it or hide your pain. I'm not afraid of it. I can handle it, and you."

Sassy gasped, her body shaking a little. Nathan sensing she was swallowing some sad feelings was one thing, but to offer an affirmation, and a promise? How did he always know how to speak to her?

"W-why do you call me Syreeta and not Sassy, like everyone else?" she asked, changing the subject before her heart jumped out of her chest and fell into his hands.

Nathan smiled. "Why do you call me Nathan, and not Nate, like everyone else?"

She shrugged. "Nate sounds like a boy, and you are most definitely a man." Sassy gasped as soon as the words were out of her mouth. She took another sip of her drink, appalled she'd spoken without thinking. Nathan laughed out loud.

"You know what? I'll take it," he replied, sipping his own float, "As for you, I call you Syreeta because it's who I want you to be with me. I know what people expect from Sassy—a smart-mouthed, quick-witted flirt who's always up for a good time, and not a long time. But I know part of your persona is a shield, so you don't get hurt again, so you don't feel weak again, so no one catches you slipping again. I get it, but I want Syreeta. I want the real you, all the time. Not the front you put up so people don't get too close."

Sassy turned to him, unable to stop the tears in her eyes. She wanted to be soft again, and feel safe again, and stay in one place for a while. But it was so hard to believe it wouldn't end up like before.

"Nathan, what are you doing to me?" she whispered. He pulled her close with his free arm, staring down at her with an intensity she'd never known, daring her to look away.

"Showing you it's safe to be Syreeta again," he whispered back and leaned down to kiss her.

An Unmatched Attraction

<u>*January 25th*</u>
<u>**Sassy**</u>

Sassy was sure she was dying. She was positive a lack of oxygen would kill you. But for the last however many minutes, she'd only been able to expel air, not take it in. It was the only thing her shaking, shivering, wrung out, body would do. Her knees were sore, her mouth open on a sob she didn't even have enough breath to push out. This was her own fault, really. She *had* challenged the man. Big mistake.

"Mmmm. Oom ummm yumm," garbled noises came from below her, and his tongue and lips continued turning her inside out. One innocent comment about his beard looking dry, and the next thing she knew, she was sitting on it, with instructions to "wet it herself if she was so concerned." Sassy may have been concerned before, but she'd been coming over his mouth for half an hour. She was sure his beard was as wet as she could get it.

"Nathan—Nathan—" his name was the only word her mouth would form, the only thing she had enough breath to say. Nathan was relentless, his tongue swiping against her swollen clit over and over; his lips sucking on her lower ones and sliding over her sensitive areas as if he were French kissing her pussy. Sassy didn't know how to resist his magic. Not his words, or the mouth they came from; not his actions or the hands performing them; not his heart, or the body housing it. She was gone over Nathan Harper, and one day, when she remembered how to breathe, she'd have to do something about it.

"Shit. Shit. Shit. Nathan, I can't—Nathan!" she screamed and held onto the headboard as her body jerked with the orgasm, she'd been about to tell him she couldn't handle. Sassy started shaking, whimpering like a cat who needed petting. *No,* she thought, swallowing more whimpers, *No more petting.* Her needy cat was how she'd gotten into this mess. Nathan moved her down, and then over next to him. He climbed between her thighs and was inside her before she could blink, and Sassy was annoyed with herself for being so preoccupied with his mouth she forgot what his dick could do. Welp. There went her breathing again.

"Syreeta, you feel like home, baby love. Can I make this my home? Can I stay here forever?" Nathan whispered to her as he moved inside her, and Sassy couldn't stop the tears on her cheeks if she tried. *Welcome home, my love,* her heart said, and it took a special kind of willpower to keep it from flying out of her mouth.

"Answer me, Syreeta. I want to come home, baby. I promise, I'll love you so good. I swear, you'll feel it every minute. I won't be him. I'd never hurt you, baby. Please let me come home," Nathan was begging her like he'd done something wrong, and Sassy was overwhelmed.

"Nathan, please—baby, I—ooooh," she moaned and cried as he filled her until there was no room. No one had ever touched her so deep inside and she was ready to keep him for the dick alone. His stroke was smooth, and so sure, so confident he knew her exact spots, that damn curve to the left caressing her walls, making her lose it, showing her there was only one man she belonged with, and only one man she should ever be opening her legs for.

"I'm sorry," she sobbed, her orgasm seizing her body momentarily, "I'm sorry I let them have what should have been yours." Sassy was babbling, but she couldn't help it. From the foot rubs after her diner shifts, to the phone calls to check on her, and notes complimenting her; from the flowers and gifts to show his appreciation for her, to the gentle way he pried her open and explored her past without making her feel broken or unlovable. Nathan was kind, caring, loving, and protective, and he was eager to be, like he'd been saving his whole heart for a chance with her. The sex was the icing on an already perfect cake, to be honest, and getting it after everything else was cracking the wall Sassy had around her heart.

"I'm sorry I didn't come for you sooner, Syreeta. I shouldn't have even given them the chance to have you. It's my fault, baby love. I hesitated, and I never will again. This is my home. Please let me come home," Nathan pleaded, and Sassy came hard, her back bowing and her eyes slamming shut. He fucked her through it, thrusting into her wetness, getting closer to his own nirvana.

"Yes, Nathan. Yes, yes, yes," she wailed, his thrusts pushing her into small aftershocks that felt like mini orgasms. Nathan leaned down, kissed her mouth, licked her tears. Then he was coming too, pumping inside her, moaning her name like a prayer.

"It took me two years to get everything I was owed. Two years of waiting tables to get by, begging and borrowing to pay my lawyer, and praying every prayer I knew. He kept harassing me, telling me I was nothing without him, sending his friends to the restaurant where I worked to rattle me and call me a gold digger. I didn't want to break him; I only asked for what was fair. I worked as hard as he did to get his business off the ground, and I did it while putting up with his verbal, and sometimes physical, abuse. All I wanted was enough to start a new life far away from him."

"And you had every right to ask for it," Nathan encouraged, rubbing her back as they lay in his huge sleigh bed. Sassy hadn't moved since they finished making love. He wiped her down, brought her water, and even put her bonnet on her hair. She was hungry, and she had no doubt he'd take care of that too, as soon as she told him. For the moment though, she wanted to continue this conversation. Nathan deserved to know what she'd been through, why she ran away from him, what she was so afraid of.

"He wanted someone to control, and as soon as I didn't want to be under his thumb anymore, he tried to punish me. The community we lived in was pretty insulated; everyone turned against me the moment he did. I was the outsider from the wrong side of the tracks he brought home and gave a better life. They thought I should have been more grateful to him, taken the bullshit settlement he offered me at first, and gone back where I came from," Sassy went on.

"But you knew you deserved more, and you fought for it. I'm proud of you, love," Nathan whispered. Sassy snuggled closer, feeling warm and content. She didn't want to move; for once she wasn't anxious to get back to her own space. She smelled like Nathan, and she didn't want to wash it off. For the first time since she showed up in Luna Lake, Sassy didn't want to run. She wanted to stay still. If she weren't so sex drunk and tired, she might be afraid, but for now, she was going to savor the moment.

"Nathan, I'm hungry," Sassy said, running her fingers over his chest. She looked up at him and he was looking down at her, grinning.

"You, my sweet, sexy, baby love, can have anything you want. Shall I go to the kitchen and report back, or do you want to come with me to see what we have?" he asked her.

"I'll come too," Sassy decided, and sat up. She looked around for Nathan's shirt and slipped it over her head. She sniffed deeply, closing her eyes with a smile on her face. Nathan pulled on a pair of pajama pants and tugged her to the edge of the bed, getting down on his haunches to roll a pair of his thick socks on her feet. Then he placed her glasses on gently, lifted her down and they left the room, going downstairs to the kitchen.

Nate

Nate lived in a two-bedroom, two-bathroom cottage right next to the water. It was painted white, with lots of windows, and a bright red door. The backyard was spacious, and he made it into another living space with lots of seating, a table and chairs under a pergola, a covered patio where his grill was housed, and a fire pit. The back deck led to a private dock, so he was the go-to host for summer parties. It was fully renovated inside, with an updated kitchen, spa bathrooms, new flooring and paint, plus all new plumbing and HVAC. Nate loved the house and planned to be there for a long time.

He'd grown up in the house, and done the renovations after his parents left it to him when they moved into town. His parents, Silas and Natalie Harper, owned two businesses in Luna Lake—a fishing supply store that sold bait, tackle, and gear, and a boardinghouse. They lived in the first-floor apartment of the boardinghouse, which was three doors down from the store. They loved being in town; they told Nate they felt isolated at the lake. But Nate liked the quiet. He liked peace. And since having Syreeta here, he liked that she could scream as loud as she wanted.

In the kitchen, he sat Syreeta at the island, and poured her a glass of water, and then a glass of wine. While she hydrated and then relaxed, he rummaged in the refrigerator and cabinet to figure out their options.

"Okay," he said, turning to her, "We can have sandwiches, hot or cold. I have lasagna from my mama, leftover smothered turkey wings I cooked last night, or we can try to catch Moonlight Over Pizza before they close."

Syreeta smiled and took a sip of her wine. "I want to taste your turkey wings, but I also want a grilled ham and cheese. Can I have both?"

Nate laughed. "Yes, baby. You can have both." He heated the turkey wings and started a pot of rice to have with it. Then he pulled out his sandwich ingredients and got to work. He made two perfect grilled ham and cheese sandwiches and then a huge bowl of turkey wings and rice for them to share.

"Is the couch okay, or you want to go upstairs?"

"The couch is fine, Nathan. I'll get us something to drink," Syreeta jumped up and poured another glass of wine for herself, and one for him. They went to the living room and settled on his sectional. Nate turned on the TV and adjusted himself, pulling Syreeta between his legs and throwing a blanket over hers. Syreeta picked up a sandwich and took a huge bite.

"Oh, this is exactly what I wanted. This is delicious, Nathan," she said around a mouthful of food. Nathan bit into his sandwich as well, savoring the buttery bread, salty ham, and sharp, melty cheese. They polished off the sandwiches in record time, and Syreeta grabbed the bowl, tearing into the tender turkey wing with a fork and scooping some rice. She offered him the first bite.

"Nah, I already know what it tastes like. I want to know what you think," he said. Syreeta popped the fork in her mouth and chewed, then turned to him with an incredulous look.

"You made this?" she asked. Nate nodded, grinning.

"It's my mama's recipe."

"Don't tell her I said this, but it's better than Ms. Minnie's recipe she serves at the diner."

"Not too many people can beat my mama in the kitchen," Nate bragged, "Pop always said if the boardinghouse meals were open to people outside, the diner and BJ's Soul Food would have a lot of competition."

Syreeta dug back into the bowl. "I want the lasagna for breakfast, then." Nate laughed and took a sip of his wine. They ate and relaxed, watching TV and settled into the intimacy of the moment.

"Why hasn't anyone snatched you up, Nathan?" Syreeta asked him suddenly, "I'm not complaining, by any means—but someone like you should have all the love you can handle. What are the women in this town missing? Or is it me who's missing something?"

Nate chuckled. He had a feeling this question would come up. "Nobody's missing anything, Syreeta. I've been involved before, and dated lots of women, in and out of Luna Lake. It's just been bad luck, and worst timing. My high school sweetheart couldn't wait to get out of this town, so she went to college out of state, and that was the end of us. Mid-twenties I was in another serious relationship, but she cheated and ended up marrying the guy. Then I was involved about eight years ago, but we grew apart because I wasn't ambitious enough for her—she had more career aspirations for me than I had for myself and made me feel like a failure for wanting to stay a barber. We parted ways. In between, I've dated casually, but nothing stuck."

"And Sabrina?"

"Bri and I were in two different places in our lives. I'm a self-aware man, baby. I work on my shortcomings; I know my triggers. I've done the work to make my life happy, and I know what I want. Bri was still figuring those things out when we were dating; it was never going to last."

"You know what you want, huh? Then, are you sure you want me, Nathan? Because it would seem we're in two different places in our lives, too," Syreeta said. She sat up in his arms and readjusted, turning her body so she could straddle his lap and look him in the eye.

"Different places? How so?" Nate questioned with a frown.

"I can't give you children, Nathan," Syreeta began, rolling her eyes.

"I don't want them, Syreeta."

"Your parents don't want grandchildren?"

"I don't base my relationship requirements on what my parents want—*I* don't want children. And for the record, my parents want whatever's going to make me happy," Nate told her. Syreeta pursed her lips, like she was thinking. He kissed her, making her mouth relax.

"Are you ready for a woman almost a decade older than you? A woman who's been passing the time with temporary lovers and has trust issues because of her past?" she pushed.

"I'm ready for *you*, Syreeta. You're who I want, and I'm ready," he insisted.

"Are you sure? I've dated around, Nathan. Other men are going to tell you they've been with me, and some of them will be telling the truth."

"We all have a past, Syreeta. Other women in this town might tell you they've been with me, and they're probably *all* telling the truth," Nate shrugged. Syreeta burst into laughter.

"My ex always made me wear a sleek, short, bob, said it was more sophisticated," she went on, her tone thoughtful, "It's why I wear my hair long now. Because I like it long. Are you going to tell me what to do with my hair?"

"I would never, baby love. I just want you happy—short hair, long hair, no hair, whatever. You're fine as fuck to me, no matter what."

"I dye these grays in the front, but one day I'll stop. You want a gray-haired woman?"

"I'm still gonna pull it when I hit you from the back and push it out the way with my tongue when I eat your pussy, no matter what color it is," Nate replied, grinning. Syreeta smirked.

"I'm perimenopausal and prone to anxiety and mood swings. Can you handle it if my sex drive changes? If sometimes I want it more, and other times I want it less? Can you handle me needing more help to get wet, and to stay aroused? Are you ready for my occasional insomnia, and my hot flashes? Because this is who I am, Nathan."

"First of all, I am ready for your body, mind, and spirit. I can and will take care of you, Syreeta. If you're ever uncomfortable with sex, we can chill. And when you want it, all you have to do is tell me. I can do whatever you need, to get and keep you aroused; our foreplay will never start or end in the bedroom. When you can't sleep, I will hold you and talk to you until you can. And you have a nightstand on your side of the bed where you can keep a fan if you need it, and lube if we need it as well. I can handle whatever you throw at me, Syreeta. I promise," Nate told her. Syreeta looked into his eyes, like she was trying to gauge whether she could believe him.

"I've never had this conversation with anyone," she confessed, snuggling closer, "My ex and I were young when we got married, and he never cared about what I wanted anyway. Once I was free of him, I stuck to temporary relationships, so the deeper shit never came up. I never had to tell anyone I had trouble sleeping because I never spent the night, and I never let them spend the night. When my sex drive changed, it simply looked like I was losing interest and it was all casual, so no one cared. But if we're going to do this, I want you to know everything. I don't want you to worry if I need a shower at 2am because I'm sweaty. When I'm not as wet, I don't want you think it's because you don't turn me on."

"I'm proud to be the man you want to teach how to take care of you. It's an honor and a privilege to be your safe space."

"See what I mean? How do you always know exactly how to speak to me?" she sighed, her eyes going soft. Nate kissed her again, tightening his arms around her.

"It's more proof this is meant to be, as far as I'm concerned," he said. Syreeta smiled, a big, beautiful smile, and Nate's heartbeat faster.

"Can we go back upstairs?" she asked. Nat nodded and they cleaned up their dishes and went back to the bedroom.

One of the first things Nate worked on after he inherited the house was the primary bedroom space. He pushed into the hall closet separating the bathroom from the bedroom, so he'd have a true ensuite. The second bathroom was on the lower level, so he deemed the upper level his private space. The second bedroom was a library, filled with all of the older classics his parents read—Hurston, Baldwin, Naylor, Walker, Hansberry, Cooper, and the like, plus all his newer favorites—Tayari Jones, Colson Whitehead, Jesmyn Ward, Jacqueline Woodson, Akwaeke Emezi, etc. Having a best friend who owned a bookstore had done wonders for his collection. Syreeta fell in love with the library, and his comfortable reading chair. She said it was a place she could disappear into, and if it got her to his home more often, Nate was okay with it.

Syreeta pulled him into the bathroom, turning on the shower and pushing his pants down. Nate took his shirt off her and grabbed a cap to cover her thick hair. He stepped out of his pajama pants and bent to take his socks off Syreeta's feet. She put her glasses on the sink, and they stepped into the shower, the heat of the water immediately relaxing them. He grabbed a loofah and his *Damani's Decadence Lemon and Cedar Body Wash*. He loved the sharp, fresh, scent, but he also had some of the *Blackberry and Rosewater Foaming Wash* in case Syreeta wanted something softer. He'd known Damani all their lives and was proud to support his business. He was happy his friend was doing something he loved and doing it successfully. Plus, the products were great and there were no shipping charges, since Damani, his grandmother, and girlfriend only lived on the other side of the lake.

Nate held the wash up for her approval and Syreeta nodded. He poured some into the loofah sponge and squeezed it, building the lather. Then he washed his baby love from head to toe. He loved her plushness, the supple parts of her that made her soft to the touch and a joy to hold. Nate didn't really know what a 49-year old's body was *supposed* to look like, but Syreeta's was perfect for him. She watched him cater to her, sighing when he touched her in a way she liked, staring at him with something like love in her eyes. Nate knew it wasn't quite love yet, but he was hoping one day, it would be. Because he was more than halfway there, and there was no going back. He knew Syreeta was the one for him; Nate prayed she would see it too.

When he was done, he went to wash himself, but Syreeta grabbed another sponge and squirted bodywash onto it.

"Let me," she said softly, and proceeded to cleanse his body in the same calm, gentle way he'd done to her. When he was scrubbed clean, they rinsed and got out, Nate grabbing two towels from the warmer and Syreeta's glasses from the sink. In the bedroom, he dried her with the same careful manner and then had her sit to the side while he changed the bed sheets. The two of them climbed back into bed, wrapped around each other. Soon, holding became kissing, and kissing became more. Nate moved on top of Syreeta, squeezing her breast lightly as he licked her fat nipples with his tongue.

"Oh, Nathan! More, please," she requested, arching up into his mouth. Nate obliged, sliding his dick up and down her slit as he licked and sucked her nipple. Syreeta spread her thighs wider, moving her hips so her clit brushed against his dick as he rocked back and forth. She was going to come like this, he could feel it. Nate kept up his movement, his dick getting slick with her arousal as he rubbed against her and tasted her nipples. Syreeta whined, her eyes shutting, and he knew she was close. Nate lifted his body and slid inside her, burying himself to the hilt. He moved his hand down and thumbed her clit, moving in a circular motion with gentle pressure.

"Nathan! Right there, baby, right there," Syreeta cried, her body arching into his. He fucked her hard and fast, taking his pleasure as he multiplied hers. She told him her clitoral orgasms were stronger and came easier, so he took full advantage, thrusting into her wet pussy, rubbing and pressing on her clit. Syreeta came again, screaming, her pussy damn near pushing him out when her release squirted out of her. Nate pushed in hard, and groaned, his nut splashing against her walls.

"Fuck, Syreeta. You're incredible," he said, his voice a harsh whisper. This woman was casting a spell on him, holding his heart, mind, and dick captive... and he didn't want to be free. He pulled out and moved to the side of her, gathering her close and rubbing her back to calm her.

"Nathan?" Syreeta whispered to him, her lips against his neck as she tried to kiss him and talk to him at the same time.

"Yes, baby love?"

"This is real... right?" she asked, her voice shaking slightly with fear and caution. Nate held her tighter.

"It's as real as it gets... and I won't let anyone take it away from us," he promised her, and the two of them fell asleep.

An Untamed Love

F "And I'm uncomfortable with all the flirting and nicknames, and shit, if we're being honest. I know it makes some of those old heads tip better, but giving younger guys all your 'Sassy' energy makes them feel like you're on the hunt, and you're not anymore."

"Nathan, it's not a big deal," Sassy insisted.

"If everyone knew you were mine, it wouldn't be," Nathan said, as he bent to put her shoes on for her, "But you decided we should go quiet after people saw us at the parade, so no one has any idea your lover position is filled—permanently."

The two of them were at her place for once, both getting ready for early morning shifts. Friday and Saturday were the two busiest days of the week at the barbershop, and it was Pancake Friday at the diner, which was probably one of Ms. Minnie's most popular specials.

"They don't need to know. I don't have to show off for anybody in this town, Nathan. They can think whatever they want about me."

"Maybe. But if they think it out loud, I'm gonna react. Long as you know, we're good," Nathan said. Sassy sighed. She knew he was right to feel a way about not being publicly claimed, seeing as she'd never hidden anyone else, she was with, but something about her relationship with Nathan made her want to protect it. As much as she was fully invested in exploring and building what she had with Nathan, it wasn't easy to turn off her fear. What if the moment she shouted it from the rooftops, it fell apart? Men tended to ruin things in her life, and Sassy didn't want to end up looking like a fool for thinking one could give her more than the limited interaction she'd expected of them after her divorce.

"I'm not him, Syreeta," Nathan interrupted her thoughts, pulling her up from the bed and into his arms, "I won't switch up on you, and as long as you keep letting me prove it, I'm good. I told you I had no problem earning your trust, so I don't expect your fear to go away overnight. But I don't want to watch you put on your 'Sassy' mask and pretend like I'm not here, and I don't think I should have to."

"You're right," she admitted, laying her head against his chest, "We've been keeping it quiet because of me, and you've accepted it, even though I know you don't like it. The least I can do is respect your position, whether other people know about it or not."

"Thank you, baby love," Nathan whispered, rocking her in his arms. After a long kiss and hug, they left her house in their separate cars and headed to work.

Sassy lived on the waterside as well, but on the opposite end of the lake from Nathan. Her cottage was cozy, but fully decked out, and her closest neighbors—Damani Roberts and his grandmother, Ms. Geneva, were wonderful people who respected her privacy, but were always there to lend a hand. Damani was in love with Jenaya Hobbs now, and they even got themselves a third: Adrian Jacobs, who, according to Ms. Minnie, had grown up in Luna Lake but moved away. Sassy saw them all at Christmas, happy and free, showing their love out loud. She wished she were fearless like them.

When she got to the diner, Ms. Minnie's car was already in the parking lot. Sassy whipped into the space beside her and went in the back door, the early morning cold pushing her feet faster. Once she was inside, she headed to the office to put her things down and as she suspected, Ms. Minnie was there, making last-minute decisions on the flavors and garnishes for Pancake Friday.

"Good morning, Ms. Minnie."

"Good morning, Sassy. Tell me something—do you think we should do chocolate chip pancakes with strawberries, or straight chocolate pancakes with peanut butter glaze instead of syrup?"

"Both of them sound too rich for my perimenopausal behind to be eating. But I like the chocolate and peanut butter idea," Sassy laughed. Ms. Minnie laughed as well.

"Thank you, honey. JB hates when I don't have my mind made up when he gets here," she said referring to the cook. He was temperamental as hell, but a genius with a spatula in his hand. He brought Ms. Minnie's recipes to life in a way no one could, except her, of course. Ms. Minnie stood up and went to the kitchen to start her pancake batters and crack eggs for JB while Sassy headed out front.

Sassy tied her apron and started prepping for opening. She turned on the lights, started the three coffee machines, adjusted the thermostat, and got some music going. Then she checked napkin dispensers, salt and pepper shakers, and ketchup bottles at all the tables. She brought out the individual syrup dispensers and turned on the POS system. Lastly, she checked the bathrooms for cleanliness, paper towels and toilet paper.

Since Ms. Minnie's daughter's Paige had left the diner to be with her husband in Atlanta, Ms. Minnie had been relying on her and Gina more and more. Sassy didn't mind. Though her divorce settlement and alimony payments ensured she didn't need the money, she loved working at the diner, and knowing she was contributing to its success. Ms. Minnie and Paige had been her first friends when she landed in Luna Lake a decade before; Sassy wanted nothing more than to be there for them the way they'd been for her. And before Nathan, working at Lakeside was a great way to scope the men in the town, and talk to them. Sassy checked on Ms. Minnie; the pancake batters were done, eggs for scrambled eggs whipped and JB had arrived and was starting on bacon. In an hour, his assistant Rafael would be there to help. Ms. Minnie gave her the nod and Sassy unlocked the front door, flicking the light switch for the sign outside, and declaring Luna Lakeside Diner open for the day.

Pancake Friday was a hit, as always, and hours later, Sassy was finally off her feet. Besides Ms. Minnie's Chocolate with Peanut Butter Glaze, they'd also served Peach Cobbler Supreme—pancakes with peach slices, topped with almond crumble and brown sugar syrup—and Classic Buttermilk with berry add-ins available: blueberry, raspberry, and strawberry. Kids had even come in with their parents before school and to-go orders were off the charts. Her, Gina, and the other two girls working were efficient and friendly, as always, but it was tiring. And she hadn't flirted with a single customer. She had Nathan, and she didn't need anything more. The bell jingled as the diner door opened.

"Sup, Sassy. Come take my order," Sharif said, sitting at the counter. Sassy shook her head. She'd had to block him when he got ignorant after Nathan's hang up at the parade. When she saw him around town, he simply sneered at her, and if he was with someone, he whispered. Sassy didn't care about him spreading rumors; she'd spent her entire life having people talk behind her back. She only hoped he would leave her alone. He didn't want her, not really, and she was confused as to why he was acting so "pressed," as the kids liked to say. Nathan didn't know about the things Sharif said, and Sassy planned to keep it that way. There was no need for him to get involved. There'd be nothing but disaster.

"Gina's working the counter. She'll take your order," Sassy replied to Sharif, breezing by and dropping two plates at a table in her section. Sharif scowled. Gina approached him, ready to take his order, but he shook his head. Sassy went back behind the counter, headed to the service window.

"Says he wants you, Sass. I'll take these for you," Gina said, pointing at Sharif, and grabbing the two plates from the service window. Sassy sighed and walked up to the counter.

"Welcome to Lakeside. What can I get you?"

"You can get me a Lakeside Special with extra bacon, for starters. Then, you can unblock me. Why you acting funny, Sass?"

"Would you like anything to drink?" Sassy replied, ignoring everything except his food order.

Sharif scowled again. "You hear what the fuck I said?"

"Yes, I heard you, Sharif. You want a Lakeside with extra bacon. Do you want a drink?"

"Don't make me embarrass you in here," he warned, "Unblock my number."

"Why are you acting like this? We're not messing around anymore; you don't need to call me. I'm not gonna let you on my phone to be disrespectful because you're angry about me cutting you off," Sassy said, trying to keep her voice down.

"Listen to me, old bitch," Sharif said, his voice a low snarl, "You think you can play me because you hopped on another dick? Your hoe ass should be happy I even wanted you—"

"Is there a problem here?" Nathan walked up to the counter and sat next to Sharif. Sassy wanted to disappear into the floor. She didn't need him to hear how Sharif was speaking to her. His disrespect was embarrassing enough.

Sharif shrugged. "If it is, it ain't your business. Me and Sass working something out."

Nathan stared at her, his topaz eyes begging for permission to intervene. But Sassy didn't want to let him. This was her past, her mess, and she didn't want to chance he'd look at her differently. She shook her head slightly, then turned away, pouring two glasses of ice water quickly. She sat one in front of each of them.

"Your order will be right out," she mumbled to Sharif and walked away. She sent Gina to take Nathan's order and went back to working the floor. When she walked by again, Sharif was getting his sandwich to go, and Sassy was relieved. She went to the cooler to grab a hard root beer for one of her tables and suddenly he was there, backing her into corner.

"Let me by," she said firmly.

"I'm coming by tonight. Have my pussy ready," he smirked. Sassy rolled her eyes.

"You don't own me, and I been done with you. Get out of my way," she said, pushing him and moving by. Sharif grabbed her arm, pulling her back.

"You old whores think you're so special? You ain't no different than a young whore," he said, getting loud. Suddenly, Sassy was pulled from Sharif's grasp, and he was on the floor, holding his wrist.

"If you ever touch her again, I will kill you," Nathan growled. Sassy rubbed his arm, trying to relax his bunched muscles.

"Nathan, I'm okay," she soothed him, "I'm not hurt. I—"

"I guess you must be the new dick she sucking," Sharif said, standing up and straightening his clothes. By this time, the entire diner was looking and Sassy wanted to melt into the floor.

"I'm not gonna fuck up Ms. Minnie's business by whooping your ass in here but say one more thing and I'll be dragging you outside," Nathan threatened. He sat Sassy on a stool at the counter and ran his hands over her, checking for injuries. Sassy wanted to cry at his care, but she was still so embarrassed. What would he think of her after this?

"You going real hard for some pussy half the town done had," Sharif said flippantly, leaving the diner. Nathan clenched his fists and followed, pushing through the diner door and grabbing Sharif by the collar. Sassy ran outside, Ms. Minnie and a bunch of patrons followed.

The two men were throwing punches, but it didn't take long for Nathan to get the upper hand. He hit Sharif in the mouth, splitting his lip and the crowd reacted. Hassan and the other barbers ran from the shop and rounded the corner, trying to get a handle on the fight. But Nathan was too angry; Sassy had never seen him so angry.

Moments later, a police cruiser showed up and Rick Wilkins hopped out, with Sabrina Harlem behind him.

"Alright, everybody back up!" Sabrina yelled, waving her baton and pushing people away. Rick inserted himself between the two men, dodging flying fists and pushing them apart.

"Enough!" he bellowed, and the two men backed off each other. Everyone quieted, and Rick pulled out his handcuffs.

"Who started this shit?" he asked. Sharif turned away, wiping his split lip and mumbling something under his breath. Nate straightened his clothes and then held his wrists out. Sassy gasped. Was he going to jail for her?

"He said something disrespectful to my... to Sassy, so I hit him. And if you and Bri disperse the crowd and he's still talking shit when you leave, I'm a do it again, so you might as well cuff me, Rick."

"Nathan, no! Rick, it wasn't his fault. It was a misunderstanding," Sassy said, coming to him with tears in her eyes. She had to stop this before he had a criminal record because of her. Sharif sneered at them, and Rick sighed. Nate looked at her, anger and disappointment in his eyes. Sassy knew what he was thinking. If she'd acknowledged their relationship, and asked for his help, Sharif might not have been so bold with her, or so disrespectful.

"If you'd have let me handle it when I wanted to, he wouldn't have even thought he could say that shit to you, Syreeta. But it's cool. Come on, Rick. Let's get this shit over with. Hass, call my pops to post my bail," Nate spat out, cutting his eyes at her and echoing her thoughts. She started to sob, and Ms. Minnie pulled her back into the diner.

"Go on home for the rest of the day, Sassy. Your shift was almost over anyway," she said. Sassy sighed. A nice hot bath sounded good. Hopefully, she could wash her humiliation away. And then, she'd check on Nathan.

Nate

Nate sat in the back of the police car, anger thrumming through his entire body. He didn't think he'd ever been so pissed off. For Sharif to think he could say those things to his woman... *his* woman! He wanted to smash his fist into the other man's face until it was unrecognizable. And for Syreeta to try to let it ride, and ignore it, pissed him off even more. It was obvious he'd spoken to her like that before. She didn't ask him for help because wanting his protection meant claiming him, acknowledging him, even if it was only in her heart, and not out loud. Nate was even angrier when he thought of it. He was in love with the most stubborn woman in the world.

Sabrina and Rick got into the car and pulled out. Bri picked up the radio. "Dispatch, this is 426. We have one perpetrator in custody and we're all clear at the diner."

"*Copy that, 426,*" the dispatcher replied. She chuckled.

"Nathan, what the fuck were you thinking?" she asked him. Nate shrugged; his gaze focused on the passing streets. He didn't want to say too much. He didn't need Sabrina in his business.

"Wasn't my fault," he sighed, "Reef got all salty cause Syreeta moved on, and he said some out the way shit to her. I didn't let it slide."

"Then why were you so angry at Sassy?" Rick questioned.

"Cause her refusal to acknowledge us publicly might be the reason he approached her in the first place. Syreeta is so fucking stubborn," Nate complained, his annoyance making him admit more than he meant to.

"She's a stubborn person you clearly love—you taking charges and shit," Sabrina laughed. Nate blew out his breath and shook his head. But he didn't deny it, because he couldn't. Syreeta Dumont was his one. His love. The only woman he wanted. He loved her, with his entire heart. She was the other half of his soul. But would she ever be healed enough to admit she felt the same?

"Keep reminding her you ain't going nowhere," Rick said, staring at him through the rearview mirror, "Sassy's scared. She needs to know you ain't gonna switch up or disappear. Take a break if you need one, but don't abandon her. If she's your heart, then stake your claim, man." Nate stared at him and then nodded his head. He'd been promising her he wouldn't switch up all along. He couldn't do it now. But he needed to know she was going to try, otherwise he was wasting his efforts.

Nate was taken into the police station and thrown into a holding cell. He wasn't there an hour before his dad showed up, ready to post bail.

"There is no bail, because no one's gonna file any charges. You can take him," the clerk said. An officer opened the cell and Nate walked out. His dad's lips twitched, as if he wanted to laugh. He and Nate walked outside and got into his car.

"Something funny, old man?" Nate asked, annoyed.

Silas Harper smiled at his son. "Tried to put somebody in the dirt behind her? She must be the one. Your mama told me to tell you to invite her to dinner."

After assuring his mother he was okay, Nate was at home, washing the day off him. Hassan told him not to worry about the barbershop. Syreeta had called, but he simply texted to let her know he was okay. He didn't want to talk yet.

Once he was clean and, on the couch, he ordered pizza and poured himself a whiskey. He had two drinks by the time the pizza arrived, and five drinks by the time he ate the entire thing. Then, he picked up his phone. Syreeta sent a heart after his last text. He called her, feeling his annoyance return.

"Nathan? Are you okay?"

"Why didn't you tell me he was bothering you? Why didn't you let me handle it when I wanted to?"

"I was embarrassed, Nathan," Syreeta said, "I didn't want you to be reminded of the people I was with before you. I'm not ashamed; my body and choices are my own, and I was a single woman. But I didn't want *you* to be ashamed and reject me. You'd be surprised how a man can switch up when his ego is bruised."

"I'm not surprised at all, Syreeta, because that's exactly what Sharif did. But I'm not him. If you keep painting me with the same brush, we're never gonna get anywhere," Nate said, trying to keep the slur out of his voice. He put the phone on speaker and sat it down, pouring another whiskey.

"I'm not painting—"

"I know how hard it is for you to step out on faith, but you know eventually you're going to have to, right? You plan to spend our whole relationship waiting for me to fuck it up?"

"No, I—"

"I can't force you to trust me, and I'll never stop waiting, because you're worth it... but when are you going to try, Syreeta?" Nate babbled, getting sadder and angrier the more he talked.

"You've been drinking, Nathan. We should have this conversation another time," Syreeta replied, and he could hear the tears in her voice.

"Hopefully, I'll still want to, baby love," he mumbled and cut off the call, sitting back against his couch and sipping his drink.

February 14th

Sassy

Valentine's Day was the worst day in the world. Sassy served breakfast to lovers and friends and parents treating their kids and she wanted to yell and walk out on everyone. It had been nearly a week since Nathan hung up on her, and he hadn't called. She called him once or twice, but the phone rang until his voicemail picked up and she refused to leave a message. He was mean, petty, and stubborn. But she missed the hell out of him. Men ruined everything.

"I'm not working the counter today; Sassy will take your order," Sassy heard Paige say to Adrian and Damani, setting down their drinks before she walked away. Paige was in town to help her mother, since two servers quit, and JB's assistant cook was sick. Antonio was in the corner, eating breakfast, watching his wife like a hawk, clearly not happy to be in Luna Lake. Sassy didn't blame him for feeling a way; he'd only had Paige to himself for a month before Ms. Minnie was calling her back, and it was Valentine's Day. Meanwhile, Paige kept sneaking glances at her husband, giving him longing looks and puppy dog eyes. She was going to have some make-up to do, but Sassy had no doubt they'd be okay. Antonio loved Paige too much to stay mad long.

Sassy approached Damani and Adrian. "Hey Sexy One and Two. What can I get for you?"

"Hey Sassy. We'll have two Morning Glories, with home fries for me and sweet potato hash for Damani. And we'll also have an order of biscuits and sausage gravy to share," Adrian said, granting her a small smile as he hurriedly spoke his order.

"We're gonna need an order of the Grits by Sea to go, as well. Thanks Sassy," Damani said still not looking up. Sassy smirked. With her reputation, she wasn't surprised they didn't want to get caught looking like they were flirting back. It was Valentine's Day after all, and they were in love with Jenaya. She was a hellraiser, and it was a safe bet there were more of her family members than Antonio in the diner. Sassy inputted their order into her electronic order pad and walked off. She sighed. If only they knew even pretending to flirt was taking everything she had. But there was no way she could walk around here, obvious about her sadness over Nathan. She was Sassy Dumont. It was unheard of.

"You just gon keep playing with the man, huh?" Ms. Minnie said, coming back behind the counter to grab someone a cinnamon roll.

"Ms. Minnie, what you talking about?"

"You'd rather fake flirt and have Jenaya Hobbs come in here, tearing up my brand-new diner cause she thinks you're after her men, than to take your behind to Nathan and work things out?"

"It's not my fault. He's being so stubborn—"

"Guess you'd know something about it, wouldn't you?" Ms. Minnie said, bending to warm the roll in the microwave under the counter, "Nate was trying to be with you three knuckleheads ago. You could have saved yourself some time, but you were being stubborn too."

Sassy's mouth dropped open. She snapped it shut, chastised. It was true. Nathan had been making it clear he was the better man for a long time.

"I—"

"He's been coming for you, repeatedly, Sassy. Maybe you'd better go to him this time," Ms. Minnie advised, getting the warmed roll and moving back out onto the diner floor. Sassy closed her eyes, took a deep breath. Nathan was all she wanted. There was no denying it. Maybe she'd better go to him this time.

Sassy served all her current customers and took a break, hurrying around the corner to *Luna Cutz*. She burst through the door, looking for one man. Her man. Everyone turned to look at her. Nathan collected money from his customer and came to the door.

"What are you doing here?" he asked. Syreeta licked her lips, nervous. She sighed.

"You didn't answer my calls. You were being mean, petty, and stubborn."

"Syreeta—"

"But I was being stubborn too," she kept talking, not even caring about everyone in the shop leaning in to listen, "You were right. I wasn't trying to trust you; I was waiting for you to prove I couldn't. I was expecting you to ruin it, to let your ego get in the way. I was painting you with the same brush. And I'm sorry."

Nathan pulled her close, his lips a breath away from hers, "Syreeta Dumont, you *are* stubborn. But you're also right. I was being mean, and petty, because I was feeling hurt. I'm sorry, baby love. Still, none of this has changed my mind. You can remain stubborn; I wouldn't have you any other way. My only job is to love you, and make sure you never regret choosing me. I'm not going anywhere, you hear me? I was coming for you," he promised.

"I know you were, because you always do. But it was time for me to come for you—it was time for me to try," Sassy said. He pressed his lips against hers, kissing her as the entire barbershop cheered and whistled. Sassy moaned into his mouth, wrapped her tongue around his, savored the flavor that was uniquely Nathan. Nothing had ever tasted so good. It almost tasted like... love.

"As happy as I am for you, Nate, we got customers!" Hassan yelled. Sassy and Nathan broke apart, laughing. Nathan went to his station and pulled something from the side. He brought over a long box from *Luna in Bloom* filled with perfect, pink, roses. Then he handed her two more boxes.

"One gift is romantic, the other is silly, but personal to us. Happy Valentine's Day, baby love," he said. Sassy couldn't hide her grin if she tried.

"Happy Valentine's Day. I gotta get back to the diner. RomCom Drive-In tonight?" she said. Luna Lake's drive-in movie showed Black love stories 24/7 through Valentine's Day weekend.

Nathan nodded, grinning. "I'll pick you up." Sassy leaned up for one more kiss and then left him getting teased by everyone in the barbershop. When she got back to the diner, she hurried to the office to drop her gifts. But she couldn't resist opening them. One box held a sweet teddy bear with an "Our First Valentine's Day," T-shirt and some perfume. *This is romantic,* she thought, *so the other box must be the silly, but personal gift.* She lifted the lid and laughed out loud. Inside the box was a handheld fan, and a bottle of lube.

Sassy knew it was Nathan's way of telling her he could handle their relationship. Sassy finally felt like maybe she could too.

"I guess there's no getting rid of you, Nathan Harper," she whispered and went to wash her hands and get back out on the floor.

New Growth

Hassan and Everly have been drifting away from each other after the loss of their baby, and frustration from outside pressure has them turning on each other rather than sticking together. Hassan has a plan to put the romance and intimacy back into his marriage, and help his wife heal. But Everly loves her husband just as much--and she has some plans of her own.

Content Warning: Pregnancy loss and mentions of past miscarriages

Inside Fears and Outside Noise

*D*ecember 29th, 2024
Everly

Pain, sharp and persistent, ripped across her belly. Everly Hobbs-Meadows moaned, holding on to the arm of the chair she was sitting in. *This can't be happening,* she thought, *I didn't even get a chance to tell him.* Tears pricked her eyes and fell down her cheeks. She recognized this pain. This cramping was almost as familiar as her husband's touch, and Everly was sickened by how well she knew it. She was losing another one.

"Ev? You in here?" Hassan came in the door and headed to her in the family room. Another sharp pain made her double over and she cried out, her tears falling harder. Her husband ran into the room, kneeling by her chair.

"Ever? Baby? What's wrong?"

"I'm sorry," she whispered, and the pain stole her consciousness.

When Everly woke up, she was in the hospital, as expected. Her husband's big body was folded into the small chair by her bed and his head was in his hands.

"Hass?" she croaked. He looked up, relief coming into his hazel eyes. They filled with tears as he stood and grabbed her hand.

"Ev, my God. You scared the shit out of me," he whispered. He grabbed a cup of water and held the straw to her lips, coaching her through small sips. When her thirst was quenched, he put the cup down and held her face in his big hands, kissing her forehead, then her nose and cheeks.

"I'm sorry, baby—"

"Everly, you don't have a damn thing to be sorry about, I keep telling you that," Hassan cut her off, pulling the chair as close to the bed as he could and sitting back down. He was holding her hand, kissing her palm. Everly loved the softness of his lips, his gentleness, his care. She loved *him*. He was the sun in her sky, which only made her inability to give him a child more painful.

"I didn't even get the chance to tell you before—Hass, why is this happening to us? Why am I broken?"

"Don't you ever say no shit like that about my wife. You are not broken, Everly. You are everything I want and need. You are my partner, and my life. I know you're upset, love, and I wish I could tell you why this happened, but you are not broken, do you hear me?"

"I can't give you what you want..."

"All I want is you. All I've wanted for the last damn near twenty years, is you. Now, let me get the doctor, baby. They need to check you out. Hopefully, I can take you home soon," Hassan said. He was comfort, a balm, a paragon of unfailing support. But then, he always was. He'd long been a person who would stand in the gaps for her, who would face a storm so she wouldn't have to. The same person he was when she met him as a child, when she married him at eighteen, and when she promised him, she'd grow his legacy in her womb. The same person he was... the last three times this happened.

Everly kissed him once more, and then he left the room to get the doctor. She sighed, her tears still falling. She twisted the ring on her finger, her thoughts plagued with failure. Everly could hear her mother and Hassan's, telling her how much they were looking forward to more grandchildren. Her older brother MJ had two kids, Ox and Trinity, and Hassan's two younger sisters had five children between them. Neither of them knew her and Hassan's "holdout" was her body's inability to hold on to her pregnancy. After the first miscarriage, the looks of pity were so gut-wrenching they knew they couldn't handle any more of them.

The only people privy to their troubles were Hassan's two best friends, his cousin Lilah and Nate Harper, who'd been cutting hair with him for years—her cousin Jenaya, and Everly's gynecologist, Dr. Barnett. Jenaya was the Chief Nursing Officer at the hospital, and she made sure they got in and out with as much privacy as possible. Luna Lake was a small town, and Everly was sure people whispered behind her back, wondered why she was too stubborn and selfish to give her husband a child. If they only knew she'd been trying with all her might.

"Everly? Oh, baby, how are you feeling?" Jenaya came into the room, closing the door behind her. She came over to the bed and gathered Everly into her arms. The tears started in earnest then, sobs shaking her entire body.

"Naya, what's wrong with me?" she beseeched her cousin for answers. At 37, she was four years older than Jenaya, and the gap led to a lot of separation as children, but as adults, the two of them couldn't be closer, especially since Jenaya was living here again. They shared secrets, hopes, and dreams; Everly was the first person Jenaya told about falling for Damani *and* Adrian, and hoping to be with *both* of them. Everly was sad when Jenaya moved off the compound and into Damani's house, but Adrian had come for Christmas and Jenaya was living her dream, so she was glad for them.

"Baby, there's nothing wrong with you, do you hear me? Nothing," Jenaya was insisting now, rubbing her back, "You are fine, and you're going to be fine." Everly cried, her chest hurting, her soul bruised. All she wanted was to give her husband a baby. A ginger, like him—with light skin, freckles, burnt orange hair, and hazel eyes. Maybe chunky, like she was, with her smile. Was it too much to ask? Everly prayed every night for a breakthrough, but the only thing breaking was her heart, over and over. She'd been with Hassan for nineteen years. Would he leave her to find a family somewhere else? Was she running out of time?

"I don't know what to do, Naya," Everly cried.

Jenaya stood up straight and sat down in the chair by the bed. She took Everly's hand, "I think we should talk to Dr. Barnett about birth control," she said softly. Everly sniffed, wiping her face.

"What?"

"I think you need to give your body a break, Ever. You've been through four of these, and you're getting older. It's not getting easier on your system, or your spirit. Give it a year, Ev—one year of you not having to think about this, to worry about this. I think it would be good for you and Hassan."

"But I'm getting older, like you said. I don't want to run out of time. I don't want to lose my opportunity."

"And I don't want to lose *you*," Jenaya insisted, "You're practically my sister, Everly. If something happened to you—"

"Naya, I—"

"Think about it, okay? Promise me you will," Jenaya begged. Everly nodded, even though she didn't want to. She wanted to figure out what was wrong with her womb, why her prayers weren't coming true. She wanted to give her husband the family he deserved.

"What if it doesn't happen, Naya?" Everly whispered, voicing her greatest fear, "What if my body can't hold on? What if we can't have a baby?"

"Then you can travel, or expand your businesses, or a thousand other things. You want to know how I spent my Christmas? Getting drunk and making love. Because I don't have kids. And if push comes to shove, there's more than one way to be a mama, Everly. You and Hass can explore your other options."

"Exploring our other options always feels like accepting my body's defeat," Everly confessed.

Jenaya scowled. "Exploring your options means finding the best way to get what you want. Nothing more, nothing less. Your body is wonderful, Ev. It's keeping you here."

"Mrs. Granger from the Ladies League said maybe if I lost some weight—"

"I'm a nurse for a living, and Mrs. Granger is a gossip. Who do you think knows more?"

"Aunt Mavis said not having a baby would cost me Hassan—"

"The only reason Aunt Mavis thinks a baby keeps a husband is because she needed a baby to even get one in the first place. You've got to shut out the noise, Everly. What does Hassan say?"

"That all he wants is me, and all he's ever wanted is me," Everly said, a small smile forming.

Jenaya grinned. "Exactly. You and your man's voices are the only ones who matter. Listen, I've got to get back to work, baby. But you take it easy for a week or so. Hass should be coming back with the doctor at any minute. Soon as he clears you, go home. And rest."

"I love you, Naya," Everly said.

"Love you back," Jenaya said and hugged her once more before leaving the room. When Everly was alone again, she laid back against the pillows, sighing deeply. Naya wanted her to take a break, and even she could admit she felt like she needed one. But wasn't it the same as giving up? She wasn't getting any younger. Plus, although losing Hassan always seemed too far-fetched to even consider, Everly had to wonder how much would be too much for him. She placed a hand over her belly. Was it time to explore her other options? And would Hassan even be open to them?

<u>*January 19th*</u>
<u>**Hassan**</u>

Hassan Meadows watched his wife tend to the flowers in the greenhouse behind their home. Her hands moved with confidence as she tilled the soil, watered, and pulled weeds. Everly owned the flower shop in town, *Luna in Bloom*, and there was no way to carry the many varieties of flowers she did without a controlled environment. The shop was gifted to her by her grandfather, Titus Hobbs, (who they all referred to as PawPaw), on her 25th birthday.

Living on the Hobbs family compound had its perks—one of the major ones being the space and land to do whatever they wanted. The house they occupied had been built as a single family but was expanded into an oversized duplex when he married Everly. Her brother Matthew, "MJ" Hobbs, his wife Tiara, and their kids—Matthew III, who everyone called "Ox," and Trinity—lived on the other side of the duplex. The same year Mr. Titus gave Everly the flower shop, he signed the house over to them, and MJ and Tiara. He told them they were free to expand and renovate as they wished. Hassan and MJ overhauled both places to maximize space, upgraded the whole design, and extended the porch all the way around. They also partitioned off space for a garden for Tiara and built Everly a greenhouse. Everly's parents, Matthew Hobbs, Senior and Dr. Ramona Hobbs, lived up the road in another house.

Hassan's family wasn't the most excited about him choosing to live on the Hobbs compound. But when he got married, he had one more year of college, and Everly was just starting; the compound provided them with stability in the first years of their marriage, and then once they were established, consistent monthly expenses beat out haggling with landlords any day. Besides, it was a great environment. For all the mess that comes with big families, the Hobbs clan took care of each other; they looked out for their own. Mr. Titus wouldn't let any of them fall if he could help it, and they returned the favor. The patriarch had a stroke the year before and the entire family came together to look after him, nurse him, and help him recover. He was doing so much better, and Hassan knew the love of his family had brought him to this point.

Hassan hopped down off the back porch and headed to his wife. Neither of their shops opened on Sunday and tomorrow was a holiday, so he was hoping he and Everly could go on a date and spend the day together.

Everly Hobbs-Meadows was a work of art, standing at five-foot-seven with flawless medium brown skin and auburn eyes. Her wide nose and bow-shaped mouth made him stare like the first time, every time. Her hair was braided down her back, but was a mess of dark curls when it was loose. She had a wonderful, plush body, plus-sized and pear-shaped, with a soft belly, wide hips, perfect breasts, and thick thighs. She was his dream girl, and his forever love.

"Good morning, Lily of the Valley," he greeted her, coming in the door. Everly burst into laughter, shaking her head. Since she loved and sold flowers, it was their private joke for him to call her whatever flower name he could think of when they talked to each other.

"Good morning, husband," she said back, and Hassan felt a weight lift from his heart just seeing her smile. It had been three weeks since the hospital, and Everly refused to talk about the miscarriage, saying she needed time to process. Hassan respected her wishes, but he couldn't help feeling left out. His favorite place to be was wrapped up in his wife, in her every thought and feeling, in her every hope and dream. He considered it a privilege to have access to her soul, and he struggled when she shut him out.

"I was hoping to have some of your attention today," Hassan asked tentatively, hoping Everly would want to be with him. He missed her.

Everly sighed. "I'm trying to do a restock at the store, honey. I have three crates of blooms to take over, and arrangements to start."

"I could help," Hassan offered, but Everly shook her head.

"I'd spend more time telling you what to do than doing it," she returned, and he swallowed his frustration. She was right—even after years of being married to her, he knew as much about flowers as she did about haircuts, which wasn't much—but still. Hassan simply wanted to be with her. Did she not see that?

"I miss you, Ev," he blurted out, deciding to be honest, "I want to spend some time with you today. I feel like we haven't... we haven't been together. Can we have dinner later?"

"I don't know how long I'm going to be at the store, honey. Maybe tomorrow," Everly hedged, picking up her shears and cutting flowers. Hassan closed his eyes and counted to ten. He didn't want his frustration to show anger. He was careful with his wife... always.

"Everly Meadows, I love you. I miss you. At least tell me what you need. I know I can't tell you how to process, or dictate a time, but I lost something too, and I'm scared I'm losing you along with it. Please don't shut me out." Hassan poured his heart out to her, because what else could he do?

"I can't handle this," Everly said, turning her back to him, "This is why I didn't want to be with you. I'm not ready to talk about this. I don't want to hold your emotions, Hassan; I can't even hold my own right now. I'm afraid to go through this again—"

"Then, let's not," Hassan said. Everly spun to face him, her brown eyes wide.

"What?"

"We don't have to talk about what happened, Ev. I'm not going to force you to confront anything you don't want to. All I want is to be with you, dammit. And if you're afraid of us ending up here again, we don't have to. We can take some time off, not think about getting pregnant. We can just... be. Let's plan a vacation, or—"

"A vacation? You're willing to give up on us being a family for a vacation?" Everly said, hurt coloring her words.

"Since when are the two of us not a family, Ev? I'm not giving up on anything. I'm trying to refocus on what we already have, baby. And I'm trying to give you a break. I know I can't relate because it's not my womb, but I see what this is doing to your body, your spirit... to the *family* of you and me. And all I'm saying is, if you're afraid, we don't have to."

"You don't want to have a baby with me?" she whispered. Hassan went to her, hauled her against him, held her tightly.

"What I *don't* want is to watch you risk your life, and your wellbeing. What I *don't* want is to lose my family. Everly, you are my entire heart, and what I *don't* want is to watch my heart break, anymore." Once he finished, his wife crumpled in his arms, her sobs loud and filled with pain. Hassan held her, rocked her, kissed her hair and whispered how much he loved her.

"I wanted to make you happy, baby," Everly bawled. Hassan held her away from him, looking into her eyes.

"Who the hell told you I wasn't?" he asked gruffly. Everly looked away, continuing to cry. Hassan pulled her back against him, cursing their meddlesome families. He hadn't even considered the pressure she must be getting from their moms and other relatives. It was pressure they never brought to him; Everly was the one who would carry the children, so they saved it for her.

"I'm sorry, love. I didn't think about the pressure you were under; the questions you were fielding. I'll take care of it from now on, okay? Don't you worry, my Peach Blossom. I got you," Hassan declared. Everly laughed through her tears like he hoped she would and held onto him so tight.

Hassan was able to convince his wife to run away with him for the day, and after packing a small bag, they got in the car and drove an hour and forty minutes away to Myrtle Beach. Everly suggested they turn their phones off and he agreed, loving her willingness to escape into a bubble with him. They walked on the boardwalk, rented bikes and cycled the local gardens; they went to the aquarium, and even played a round of golf. They ate as much as their stomachs would hold, and Hassan followed his wife around the outlets, swiping his card where she told him to and carrying her bags. When they made it home, they showered and fell into bed, sleeping soundly in each other's arms.

January 20th

The next day, Hassan was anxious to keep things romantic and easy with him and Everly. He knew there were tough conversations ahead, but he wanted his wife to see there was no need to feel like she was lacking in any way, and no need to feel like they couldn't be a family on their own or have children another way. On the other side of the hard conversations were plenty of options, but he needed Everly in a good enough place to get to them. Which was why he made her breakfast in bed, on the advice of his cousin Lilah, loaded her crates of flowers in his truck and sent her off to the store to do her restock. One of her cousins would meet her at the store to help her unload.

After she left, Hassan took their rarely used second car and went to his grandfather's estate on the west side of town. His family was scattered all over Luna Lake, but his parents still lived with his grandfather, along with his cousin Harry, his great-aunt Lillian—his grandfather's sister, and a couple of other relatives. He parked and went inside, yelling out for whoever was home. There was a good amount of family at the house, mostly congregated in the kitchen and spilling over into the family room. Hassan spoke to everyone and sat at the kitchen island, watching his mom cook. His two sisters were helping her, and they each got a hug before getting back to work.

"Hey Mama."

"Hey, my son. What's going on witcha?"

"Got some things on my mind. I need to ask y'all something," Hassan said.

"Go ahead, baby. Ask me what?" Simone Meadows turned to her only son with an encouraging smile. She was darker than him—he inherited the light skin and ginger hair common among the Meadows clan—but he did have her nose and ears.

"Have any of y'all been talking to Ever about us having kids? Asking her why we don't have them yet, telling her we need them, or I won't be happy without them, anything like that?"

"I ask her what she's waiting for all the time," his sister Samirah admitted, "I mean, she's not as old as you, but she's getting up there."

"Plus, we know you want kids, Hass. You love them. Sometimes people need a nudge, you know?" his sister Saniyah put in. Hassan rolled his eyes.

"My wife doesn't need a nudge. She's getting too much pressure from too many people, especially people she thinks are speaking for me. I'd love it if you'd leave her alone about children. We know what's best for us, and I don't want Ever feeling like she has to live up to some expectation put on her by people who *think* they know what I want. My wife is more important than anything."

"For the record, I was speaking strictly for myself. But seriously, are you two ever gonna give me grandchildren?" Simone asked, and Hassan frowned.

"Maybe we will, maybe we won't. But whatever we do will be on our own time."

"What, did Everly tattle on us or something?" Samirah smirked.

Hassan narrowed his eyes. "She didn't have to. You think this is a game, Mirah? Leave my wife alone. If I find out anybody's been poking and prodding her about kids, you're gonna answer to me. And then you won't see me. I'll walk away from anything and anyone to have Everly."

Samirah frowned and turned away, and Hassan knew she was hurt he was reprimanding her.

"Hassan, wait a minute," his mother said, turning from the stove. She came over to him, wiping her hands on a towel, "You're serious, aren't you? We weren't trying to make Everly feel bad or anything. You know we meant well, don't you?"

"It doesn't really matter what you meant, Mama. Everly's feeling pressured, and that has no business being the case. I'm happy with my wife and satisfied with my marriage. Implying I'm not because she hasn't had a baby yet is inappropriate, no matter how well-meaning you are."

"I'm sorry, brother," Saniyah spoke up, "I'll apologize to Everly too, if you want. It's insensitive to mind someone's womb, and I admit I'd forgotten how it feels. Damon's mother was all over me about kids before we had them. She used to come and pray over my stomach, and send me 'healthy womb,' concoctions. She was doing so much, when we finally did get pregnant, Damon was worried I was only doing it to shut her up."

"Niyah, why didn't you tell me?" Simone Meadows questioned her youngest daughter.

Saniyah smirked. "Because I know how you are, lady. She was out of pocket, yes, but she's still my mother-in-law. Besides, I have a good husband. Damon checked her. Kinda like your son is checking you right now." She giggled and went back to peeling potatoes and Hassan kissed the top of her head. His mother rolled her eyes.

"Okay, okay. You're right. I am sorry, my son. Bring Everly to dinner so I can apologize to her too. I love that baby; she's like my own daughter. I don't want her to feel like she's failing some test. She's your wife."

Hassan nodded. "We'll come for dinner, soon. And thank you, for understanding. I appreciate you listening." Saniyah and his mother nodded. Samirah didn't say anything, but Hassan wasn't too worried. She was pouting, but he'd passed the torch of giving in to her every whim to her husband. He had his own wife to indulge. He hugged the three of them, then ventured into the family room to see what everyone else was getting into.

A couple of hours later, Hassan was heading back to the compound. He was hoping to speak to his in-laws about backing off as well, and then he needed to go check on his wife, and his cousin

Lilah, who insisted on opening her bookstore today. As he got out of the car in front of his in-law's house, the door opened and Everly's mother waved at him.

"Hey, Son," she greeted, with a smile on her face. Dr. Ramona Hobbs had passed everything but her eyes onto her baby girl—same pear shape, same medium brown skin, same mess of dark curly hair. But Mama Mona usually reined hers in for work—she was the principal of Luna Lake High School. Today, it was loose, dancing on her shoulders as she hugged him tightly and ushered him into the house.

"How you doing, Mama?" Hassan said.

"I'm fine, honey. How's Ever? I heard she's been sick. I've been meaning to come and see her, but school reconvened, and we hired a new band teacher and things have been hectic."

"I heard about the new band teacher. Ox and Trin said they love her already. But Ev is fine, Mama, and feeling much better. I actually came here to talk about her, if you have a minute."

"I always have a minute for my favorite son-in-law," Mama Mona said, laughing at her own joke. He was her only son-in-law. They sat down in the den.

Hassan cleared his throat. "Have you been mentioning kids to Everly? Asking her when we're gonna have some, telling her we need them?"

Ramona Hobbs frowned. "Yes, sometimes I do. Nothing serious, just small jokes here and there. Did she say I was pressuring her?"

"No, Mama. But that doesn't mean she doesn't still feel pressured, if you catch my meaning. I've been noticing her shifts, and I think even though folks might mean well, Everly is feeling like she's failing me, or failing us, because we don't have kids."

"My poor baby girl," Mama Mona said, "I had no idea. Nothing about the way you two love each other could ever be a failure and I'm sorry, son. I'm sorry for contributing to something like this. A person's womb is above all things, their business, and I should have been more sensitive."

"Thanks, Mama. I appreciate you hearing me out. I didn't want to overstep, but I have to protect Ev. It's my most important job," Hassan said. His mother-in-law hugged him.

"I knew you were perfect for her," she whispered. Hassan smiled. They spent a bit more time talking, and then he left, feeling confident he'd gotten through to his family. Now, it was time to check on his wife.

Romance 101

J<u>*anuary 31st*</u>
   <u>*Everly*</u>

Everly hummed as she packed another arrangement. It seemed love was in the air already in Luna Lake, and especially among her circle of friends. Aislin Ross, the new band teacher, had called in an arrangement for Lilah, Hassan's cousin, who owned the bookstore. Nate Harper ordered a huge bouquet for Sassy Dumont, with the cutest personal note. Then Adrian Jacobs called all the way from Baltimore to order flowers for Jenaya, saying he missed her and wanted to feel closer to her since it would be Valentine's Day before he saw her again. He said he trusted her to put together something her cousin would love, and Everly was honored. She knew how much Jenaya loved him and hoped they would all work out the long distance.

"Hello, my beautiful Iris," her husband said, walking into the shop with a bag in his hands. Everly giggled, flowers falling from her hands and onto the counter.

"Hassan," she chided, but she loved it. It was the corniest joke, but it was theirs, and this man of hers never forgot it.

He walked up to the counter, sitting the bag down. "What? You wanna be a Daisy today?"

Everly shook her head, grinning. "Why can't I be Everly, today?"

"In front of people, you can be all the Everlys you want to be. When it's us, you're my Perfect Peony, and this is my way of honoring what you love."

"You're what I love," she whispered, looking up into her husband's huge hazel eyes. He was a beautiful man, his light brown face dotted with freckles, thick lips tilted in a smile, his reddish-orange hair cut low and perfect, thanks to Nate. He was the only person Hassan let cut his hair and Hassan was the only person Nate let line up his beard, since he was bald.

Hassan leaned forward and pressed their lips together, and the room spun a little. Everly dropped the rest of the flowers and leaned up on her toes, wanting more of his flavor. The kiss deepened and she moaned, letting his tongue sweep her mouth. Everly gave him her tongue back, licking and sucking on his mouth.

"I'm a put up the 'Closed' sign and take you in the back, keep playing," Hassan growled against her lips. Everly giggled and moved back, her nipples hard and her panties damp. Nineteen years and the effect this man had on her was still instant, and still powerful.

They hadn't made love since the miscarriage, but Hassan was still affectionate, and loving, while respecting her need for space. They had been doing a lot of much needed talking. He told Everly about getting their families to back off, and she cried in his arms, overwhelmed because her husband would do anything to protect her, and he proved it every day. Then, both her mother and his invited her to lunch, where they apologized for their jokes and intrusive questions about having children. It was more than Everly expected from either of them, and it only made her love her husband more.

She and Hassan explored their history of trying for a baby and realized somewhere down the line, things turned from wanting to expand their family, into wanting their family to *look* like everyone else's. Everly was also able to admit that being a Hobbs, and marrying a Meadows, caused her to put undue pressure on them to add to the big family environment they grew up in.

"You taking a break, love?" Everly asked her husband now. Hassan nodded and opened the bag he brought in with him. As soon as he lifted the container, she smelled the sweetness of chocolate, and she knew what he'd brought her. She grinned.

"I am. And I thought we could break together, with a couple of these," Hassan lifted the lid of the container and Everly licked her lips in anticipation. He had two perfect, White Chocolate Raspberry Donuts. *Luna Sweets*, the town bakery, loved to experiment with desserts, and this was a popular item for them, A light, fluffy, donut, filled with raspberry jam and topped with white chocolate glaze, candied raspberries, and white chocolate shavings. It was decadent, and delicious. Her husband knew her too well. Being surrounded by blooms all day, Hassan knew there was never a need to bring her flowers. But dessert? He could always bring dessert.

Everly gestured to a stool against the wall. "Come sit with me," she invited. Hassan brought the chair around the counter and sat next to her, reaching for one of the donuts as she reached for the other. Everly took a big bite, loving the sugar rush, the smooth sweetness of the chocolate and the slight tart of the raspberries. She chewed happily, dancing in her chair.

Hassan laughed. "I knew this was the right thing to do. It's a perfect start to my plans."

"Plans?" Everly asked, with a mouthful of donut. Hassan nodded, laughing before he took a bite of his own food.

"In two weeks, it will be Valentine's Day. And I decided to take it back to basics. The next two weeks will be Romance 101. I'm going to remind you why you fell for me, Ev. I'm gonna show you why we're perfect for each other, baby or no baby. And this is the first step."

Everly stared at him, her eyes welling with tears. Her husband was an incredible man, and she was so blessed, she could barely believe it. He wanted to romance her; to remind her they were soulmates. It was the most loving thing she'd ever heard.

"Oh, Hass... you're so amazing, baby. But I don't need—"

"Yes, you do," he insisted, leaning over to kiss her and lick the chocolate from her mouth, "You're my Rose, my Daffodil, the only flower in my garden, and I have to water you, Ev. I have to be present with my love, so you know why you should keep choosing me after all this time," he said, his eyes pleading with her. Everly was blown away by his declaration, but a little sad that her husband wasn't confident she'd choose him, every day. The miscarriages created a distance she hadn't tried to lessen, and now he was unsure. Everly sighed. There was no reason to be. Her heart would never belong to anyone else.

"Hassan, you're a dream come true," she whispered. He smiled at her, kissing her once more. He pushed the rest of his donut over to her.

"I'm a man who loves his wife," he shrugged, "Finish your dessert. It'll make you smile. I remember when we first started dating, making you smile was all I wanted to do. And once I figured out how much you loved sweets, it was easy."

Everly kissed his cheek and leaned into him, finishing her donut and his while he held her, and kissed her hair.

Later, Hassan was back at work and Jenaya came in to get her flowers. Everly intended to deliver them, but her cousin had some other stops to make on Main Street and told her not to bother.

"These are so beautiful, Ever. Thank you," Jenaya said, picking up the crystal vase with the huge arrangement.

"Thank your guy. Adrian was adamant you needed something to brighten your day," Everly said back.

Jenaya sighed. "He probably did it because I cried on our call last night. I miss him so much, Ev. I can't wait until he gets back here."

"I'll bet you can't. And he obviously can't either. How's Damani doing?"

"He's great. He's still my perfect lover man, you know? We're just better when we're three. And all of us know it. How's Hass?"

"Still my perfect lover man," Everly echoed her cousin's sentiments, "He brought me donuts and took a break with me today. Then he told me we're going back to basics."

"Meaning what?"

"He wants me to remember why I fell for him, why we still belong together. He says the next two weeks leading up to Valentine's Day are going to be Romance 101. He wants to learn me all over again."

"And I thought *my* guys were sweethearts. Wow, Ever. Hass is still keeping the flame burning after twenty years. How do you feel? Are you happy?"

"I am, but I never stopped choosing Hass. I never stopped wanting him. I just couldn't see past how hung up I was on having a baby. And I still think I want one, but it's been so nice not obsessing over it. He understands that too, and he's never wavered. Hassan protects me, even when I can't see anything but myself. He doesn't have anything to prove to me. I love this idea of his, and I love romance, but I hate thinking of him doing this because he's not confident in how I feel about him," Everly expressed. Jenaya stared at her thoughtfully.

"Then maybe Romance 101 can be a class you both take," she said.

Everly frowned in confusion. "What do you mean?"

"I mean, he's dialing up the loving, so why can't you? For every lesson Hassan gives you in how well he listens and cares, give him one back. Show him what *you've* learned after nineteen years. If you're worried he's not confident in how you feel, reinforce it so he is," Jenaya shrugged after she finished, and Everly smiled. It was perfect. And she knew exactly how to start.

February 1st

Hassan

Hassan woke up feeling optimistic about his marriage, his life, and his plans for Everly. They were both early risers, and their businesses opened early as well. Plus, Saturday was the busiest day of the week for both of them. But that wouldn't stop Hassan from starting his plans to get back to romance basics with his wife.

When they first started dating, he would leave notes in Everly's bag or jacket pockets, short missives wishing her a good day, or telling her he couldn't wait to see her. Everly loved reaching into her pocket and pulling out an affirmation of his love; Hassan loved seeing her smile. This morning, he left a travel mug of coffee and a warm croissant on the counter for his wife, and then he stuck a note into her jacket:

Have a wonderful day, Azalea. I love you. See you at home ;)

Hassan left the house and hopped into the car with Nate. They rode together most mornings, since they opened the shop at 7am, and were the only two barbers there until 9.

"Sup?" he spoke, fastening his seatbelt. Nate gave him the head nod and pressed the gas, taking them back out of the compound and on the main road. Hassan sat back, sighing. He hated getting out of his warm bed. Everly was snuggled against him all night, her softness soothing him into sleep. There was no space between them in bed anymore, which Hassan knew was a sign she was feeling better. They weren't making love, but he could wait; he just wanted her to be comfortable and settled again.

"I think LJ's got it bad for the new band director," Nate said, smirking.

Hassan chuckled. "Yeah, I do too. She wasn't interested in anything but her store and those books. Now, when we talk, she recaps her conversations with Aislin like they're basketball highlights."

"I'm wary of new people—she's my LJ—but she seems happy, so I'm good," Nate continued. Hassan nodded in agreement.

"She's *our* LJ... and I'm with you. But I think this might be good for her." They continued driving, each in their own thoughts. Lilah Jean was their best friend, besides being Hassan's cousin, and they were fiercely protective of her. The only other woman he was more solicitous with was Everly. And even with him focused on reconnecting with his wife, and Nate dating Sassy, he and Nate still agreed LJ was theirs to protect.

They were at the shop in minutes and Nate unlocked the security gates and pushed them aside. Hassan pulled his keys from his pocket to open the front door, and a piece of paper fluttered to the ground. He turned the locks and then picked the paper up, going into the shop with Nate behind him. Nate turned on the lights and started getting things ready. Hassan went to his chair, unfolding the piece of paper. There was a note written in his wife's delicate cursive:

Have a wonderful day, my husband. I love you. I miss you already :)

Hassan grinned, happiness lighting up his body. Apparently, his wife had the same idea he had. It felt good, knowing she was thinking of him too. *It's definitely a wonderful day now*, he thought, and started helping Nate get things ready.

February 6th
Hassan

Hassan whistled a nonsense tune as he swept up the shop and put things away. They were closed, and soon he would be on his way to his love. He was going to walk up the street and around the corner to his wife's shop and drive them home, since she had the truck with her. He hoped she loved the romantic activity he had planned for the day.

Hassan had been doing this less than a week, and his favorite thing by far was the way Everly matched his energy. Everything he did had her doing something just as thoughtful for him, and as much fun as he was having romancing his wife, he was having even more fun being romanced *by* her.

On the second, he dialed up the nostalgia and cooked the first meal he ever made for her—chicken tenders and French fries—and Everly was so pleased, she called up the road to her parents' house and demanded a slice of her mother's chocolate chess pie especially for him (Mama Mona usually hid when she made them and only shared them with her husband). Hassan was in heaven, lounging on the couch, eating his exclusive pie while his wife rubbed his head and ears.

On the fourth, he took her to *Melodies* after work—Everly loved live music, and attending a show or concert of some kind was how they'd spent their first ten anniversaries. After their tenth, they started trying to have a baby, and the celebrations got smaller and smaller as they struggled. Hassan told her that while he knew they couldn't turn back the clock, he wanted to get back to the things they enjoyed, to tap into those feelings and make new memories. Everly agreed, and in return, she arranged for them to take new family photos, something they also used to do every anniversary. Hassan knew the photos were a big thing for her, because the longer they were only the two of them, the less she wanted to take them, until they simply stopped. He was so grateful to his wife, and in awe of her bravery.

Tonight, was Line Dance Thursday at *Bottoms Up*, Luna Lake's most popular local watering hole. Hassan planned to learn some new moves with his beautiful wife and maybe play a game of pool while they got tipsy and gorged themselves on bar appetizers. It was another thing they used to do all the time, and he missed seeing his Everly free, and feeling good. This activity wasn't a surprise, because Hassan knew Everly would want to put on a cute top, and makeup, and fix her hair. Not giving her time to get dolled up would have taken the fun out of it, and he didn't want to mess things up.

He finished shutting down the shop and left, locking the doors and then pulling the security gates in place. Hassan walked to his wife's shop quickly, suddenly anxious to see her. His hands tingled as he thought of holding her; his breath quickened when he thought of her kiss. His heartbeat faster, and he sped up his steps. When he got to *Luna in Bloom*, Everly was laughing with someone as she rang up two bouquets of flowers for them. Hassan entered the shop, standing by the door to let the man out once he finished his transaction. He left, and Hassan locked the door behind him.

"Hi, my husband," Everly spoke, smiling wide as she started shutting down the register. Hassan walked toward the counter, smiling as well.

"Hi, my beautiful Crocus," he said, knowing he would impress her.

Everly giggled. "You've never called me a crocus before," she noticed.

"Learned some new flowers, and thought I'd show off a little," he bragged.

"They're actually some of my favorites, so I love the way you're switching it up. I'll be ready to go in about twenty minutes, okay?"

"Take as long as you need, baby. I'm here to wait for you," he promised. Everly smiled again and started straightening potted plants on shelves, wiping down displays of vases and flowerpots, and swapping wilted blooms from arrangements. Hassan got the broom and swept up stray petals, soil, and leaves. Then Everly ran her steam mop over the floor. He waited while she went into the bathroom and changed. When she came out again, Hassan grinned. Everly was sexy as hell. She'd changed into a cream-colored low-cut sweater and the tightest jeans he'd ever seen her wear. Her breasts pushed out of her top and the jeans looked painted on. Her eyes were dusted with some glittery eyeshadow, her cheeks were rosy, and her lips were glossy.

"Gotdamn," he whispered, and whistled lowly. Everly giggled, coming to kiss him on the cheek. Hassan helped her with her jacket, and they left after hitting the lights. He secured the gate in front, and they got into the truck.

"We haven't been out like this in so long," Everly observed.

Hassan nodded. "I know, baby. I'm gonna make it a habit again." He drove the short distance to *Bottoms Up*. After parking in the lot, the two of them headed in. The bar was run by Everly's uncle, Elias Hobbs and his wife, her Aunt Vangie (Evangeline). They sat right at the bar amid the action, and mostly everyone spoke to them.

"Is that my Ever?" Vangie Hobbs said, coming around the bar to wrap her niece in her arms, "I never see you in here, anymore."

"Hi, Aunt Vangie," Everly said, hugging her back. His wife was beaming with happiness, and she took Hassan's breath away. Vangie hugged him next.

"You been hiding my girl?" she demanded.

Hassan shrugged. "I sure have. I want her all to myself, and I make no apologies. Have you seen her?" He knew once his plans moved to more public outings, people would be asking why they hardly ever stepped out anymore. There was no way he would imply Everly was to blame or let her assume the blame. She stared at him now, her eyes filled with love.

Vangie laughed. "Guess I can't blame you. What can I get y'all?"

"A Chardonnay for me, and a double of Macallan, neat, for my husband. And our tab is on me tonight, Aunt Vangie," Everly spoke up, winking at him. Vangie nodded and went back behind the bar. The Hobbs family members all shared a tab at the bar.

"Ev, I can pay—"

"Nope. not tonight. You got me out of the house, and excited about drinking, dancing, and being with you. You've been patient and so loving. And you still look at me like I'm the sexiest woman in this bar—"

"You are baby."

Everly laughed. "My point is, you always *see* me, Hassan. You see me so well, and protect me even better. And I want us to romance *each other* tonight."

"Everly Meadows, I love you," Hassan said sincerely, reaching up to stroke her cheek. She sighed, and leaned into his touch, her eyes closing.

"I love you too," Everly whispered, opening her eyes again, "You didn't have to shield me like you did with Aunt Vangie. Thank you for that."

Two drinks hit the bar, interrupting their intimate moment, and they toasted to a good time. After the drinks, they hit the dance floor off to the side and got lost in the music until the line dancing started. Two more drinks for each of them, and they were in formation, moving together and laughing at their missteps. Soon, Hassan sat them down so his wife could eat. They ordered all the bar's best appetizers—fried pickles, sweet and spicy wings, potato skins, and their most popular snack, cheeseburger popcorn. It was popcorn popped in beef tallow, to give it a meaty, smoky, flavor, then tossed in cheese and drizzled with spicy ketchup. It sounded weird, but it was a sweet, savory, sticky, spicy, cheesy hit at the bar.

Everly stuffed her face, tipsy and happy, and Hassan was so filled by her obvious joy he could have floated away. The look in his wife's eyes was a look he thought died long ago and to see it again made his heart race.

"Y'all up for a double date, or should we leave you alone?" Lilah said, coming over to the table. She was holding Aislin's hand and the woman was smiling shyly.

Everly clapped her hands. "No, come sit down. Hug me, Lilah. I feel like it's been forever. And you must be Aislin, right? My mama says you're a miracle worker. How are Ox and Trin doing? We live next door, and I hear them practicing every night." Hassan and Lilah laughed; Everly was much more animated when she was drunk. Lilah hugged them both, then she and Aislin sat down. The ladies chatted while he added more food to the order, and drinks for the ladies. He'd switched to water so he could drive home. Soon, the table was overflowing, as a server dropped off sliders, loaded nachos, pretzels with beer cheese, and more drinks.

Another couple of hours, and Hassan called it a night. His wife was giggly and tipsy, unable to keep her hands off him the entire ride home. He was in heaven, savoring her touch. He couldn't deny Everly was the sexiest when she was uninhibited like this, and he wanted to make love, but he wanted the first time with his wife since the miscarriage to be when she was fully present, so he would wait.

"You have a good time, my Marigold?" he asked softly. Everly giggled.

"I love marigolds, and I love you, husband," she said back, her eyes closed as she held his thigh.

"I love you too, wife. Did you have a good time?" he asked again.

"Oh, yes," Everly replied, nodding slightly, "I forgot the food was so good. I'm gonna ask Uncle Elias to make me my own sticky wings. They were delicious. Oh, and I told Lilah you'd grill steaks for her and Aislin tomorrow. They're having a Date Night at home, and you know she'll hurt herself trying to use the grill alone. Steak sounds good, doesn't it, baby? I want steak too."

Hassan laughed at his drunk, chatterbox, wife. He loved her so much. This night couldn't have gone any better. He was able to have fun and romance his wife, and also feel like she was romancing him. They were working their way back with the simple things, and he vowed to keep it going, so they'd never get so far away from who they were ever again.

"I will grill the steaks for Lilah, and then I will come home and grill some for us. Why don't we invite MJ and Tiara to eat with us? I'll put on some chicken for the kids and make a little seafood salad."

"Perfect," Everly murmured and went silent.

Hassan kept driving, his thoughts drifting. He was glad they were getting back to themselves, but he didn't know the solution to the baby problem. He knew he'd be happy whether they had children or not. He wanted Everly to get to that place too, the place where there was no pressure. He wondered if she'd ever want to adopt, or at least foster, so they could have a glimpse of parenthood. Hassan made a note to mention it to her.

He pulled up to their house and got Everly out of the car before she fell asleep. Hassan made her swallow two aspirins and drink an entire bottle of water, then he washed her face, undressed her, and put her in bed. By the time he was undressed and beside her, she was asleep. But as soon as he turned out the light, she sought his warmth, moving right over into his arms. Hassan held her tightly and fell asleep with a smile on his face.

Love in Bloom

February 12th
Hassan

Today was going to be another wonderful day of romance. Hassan started with a loving note in his wife's jacket, and special delivery of her favorite coffee. The fast-food places and Ms. Minnie's diner all served coffee, so the closest thing Luna Lake had to an actual specialty coffee shop was Lilah's cafe above her bookstore. Everly loved their Cinnamon Toast Latte, so he stopped at *The Neverending TBR* and bought her one. He also picked up a couple of books on coping with pregnancy loss, and a grief journal to give her. When he got to Luna in Bloom, Everly was switching out display arrangements and starting the premade arrangements for her Valentine's Day specials. When he gave her the gifts, she cried and jumped into his arms, kissing him over and over. She thanked him again for always seeing her, and Hassan couldn't have been more honored.

This evening, Hassan was picking up dinner from *Luna Lakeside Diner* and taking his wife to their special spot on the lake for a night picnic. They hadn't been in years, since they were newlyweds, but it was the perfect place to eat, talk, stargaze, and kiss under the moonlight. The spot was just beyond Nate's lakeside property and secluded. There would be no interruptions, not even from Nate, since he was being antisocial and grumpy because he missed Sassy.

Hassan knew Nate's fight with Sharif at the diner and the arrest after was the catalyst for why they were into it, but he was hoping they made up soon. Nate's attitude was horrible.

"Hey Mr. Hass, I have a delivery for you," Freddie Taylor walked into the barbershop. Everyone turned to look at him, and Hassan looked up, surprised. Freddie was the local delivery guy for everyone, taking things back and forth around town for anyone who reserved his services. He did food deliveries for Ms. Minnie and BJ's Soul Food, plus a host of other businesses, including book orders for Lilah (who employed his brother Frankie in her cafe) and flower orders for Everly. But Hassan couldn't remember ordering anything.

"Delivery from who, Freddie? You need help bringing it in?"

"Your wife, sir. And nah, I'm good." Freddie opened the door fully and wheeled in a cart full of potted plants. The boys and men in the shop stared curiously, and Hassan smiled. She always told him he needed plants to brighten up his space, and he told her he had no idea how to add them to the decor.

Shakira Harlem, his sole woman barber, smiled. "Ev is whipping us into shape. I like it."

"It ain't about to get all girly in here, is it?" Old Bunchy Thomas grumbled.

"They're plants, not bows and pink butterflies. Simmer down, old man," Nate said. Hassan smirked. Coming to his wife's defense was as second nature for Nate as it was for him.

"Is she coming to place these, or are they supposed to sit in the middle of the floor?" Hassan asked Freddie. The young man grinned.

"I'm doing the placing myself," he said proudly, pulling a piece of paper from his pocket, "Ms. Everly drew me a picture of your layout and told me where everything should go." After that, he got to work, placing the plants and naming them as he went along. He put an Areca Palm by the door, and two more framing the big front window. Then he put Devil's Ivy on the shelves with the hair products that lined the back wall, and a dracaena on the small table next to the loveseat. Lastly, he placed a small potted Monstera Deliciosa at everyone's station, and gifted Shakira two extra—aloe vera plants in beautifully decorated pots.

After he was done Freddie had Hassan sign for the delivery and went on his way. Hassan went back to his customer, unable to stop smiling. He loved this gesture. It was like being able to look around and see his Everly during the day. It was a window into her heart, and he knew how much it meant to her for him to trust her vision.

Hours later, Hassan left Nate to close the shop and went to Lakeside to pick up part of their dinner. He loved the new look of the diner, courtesy of massive renovation after Ms. Minnie won the lottery months ago. He wondered if she would keep working herself. Hassan understood it was her business, but she certainly didn't have to. Then again, Ms. Minnie probably didn't trust anyone since Paige was gone. Paige, Ms. Minnie's daughter, had recently revealed her secret relationship and marriage to Everly's cousin Antonio, and left to be with him in Atlanta after years of long distance. Hassan felt bad for Ms. Minnie, but he understood Paige. Separated from your love for years? He couldn't imagine.

When he got to the diner, Sassy was at the counter. She was giggling at some guy's joke, but Hassan could see the sadness in her eyes. *She's faking hard*, he thought, *whatever's going on between her and Nate is tearing them both up.* When Sassy saw him, she swallowed her laughter and straightened up, wiping the counter. She probably didn't want it getting back to Nate that she was acting like nothing was wrong and smiling at other men. But Hassan wasn't there to report back to him. The two of them had to figure this out on their own.

"Hey Hass. What can I get you?" she asked lowly.

"He's got some dinner we're keeping warm in the back. I'll be right there after I box it up," Ms. Minnie yelled, dropping two plates on one of the tables and heading to the kitchen. Minutes later, Ms. Minnie came out with two bags and handed them to him.

"Thank you, Ms. Minnie," Hassan said, bending to kiss her cheek. Ms. Minnie smiled.

"You go on, now," she shooed him away. Hassan laughed. He threw Sassy a smile and left. His next stop was the boardinghouse. It was run by Ms. Natalie Harper, Nate's mother. She and his father Silas lived at the boardinghouse too, and Mr. Silas ran a fishing supply store.

Ms. Natalie was waiting at the curb for him. She handed him a picnic basket.

"Minnie ask you why you only wanted chicken and biscuits?" she asked, smirking.

Hassan laughed. "Nah, she didn't ask. Thanks, Auntie. I appreciate this." Hassan asked Nate's mother, who most agreed was the best cook in Luna Lake, to make him some sides to go with the fried chicken he picked up from Lakeside. Hassan was happy Ms. Minnie didn't ask why he only ordered chicken; she got an attitude whenever anyone brought up Ms. Natalie's cooking. He didn't blame her; if Ms. Natalie ever wanted to cook for anyone besides her boarders and family, she could probably put the diner and BJ's Soul Food out of business.

Hassan got to Everly's shop just as she was pulling the security gate over the front door. She made sure it was locked, and hopped in the truck, kissing him on the cheek. Hassan put the truck in Park and turned, grabbing her and kissing her deeply. Their mouths and tongues meshed , tasted each other, and Everly moaned.

"Thank you, Poppy," he whispered, his mouth still brushing against hers, "The shop looks so good."

"You're welcome, husband. I wanted to show you I was thinking about you and also follow through on something I said I would help you with long ago. Did Freddie do okay?"

"He was perfect, and pretty proud of himself after he was done," Hassan said. Everly relaxed and leaned back, smiling.

"I smell something good. Did you pick up dinner for us?" she asked. He nodded and put the truck in Drive, pulling away from the curb.

"I did, and we're going someplace special to eat." He drove quickly but carefully, rubbing Everly's thigh. She leaned back in the seat, relaxed and loving his touch. When he got to their spot and he parked the truck, she sat up straight.

"Oh Hass," she whispered, "I can't believe it. We haven't been here in—"

"Too long," he finished, getting out of the truck and coming around to open her door. He lifted his wife off the seat and onto the ground, then opened the backseat and got the picnic basket, two blankets, and a small stepstool. Everly's eyes widened with pleasure, and she took the stool from him, taking it to the bed of the truck and using it to climb in. She held out her hands for the blankets and spread one on the truck bed for them to sit on. Hassan handed her the basket and climbed into the truck bed himself. There was already a charged space heater back there, and the truck bed was fitted with LED lights. As soon as he was sitting on the blanket, Everly crawled into his lap.

"A picnic! I have the best husband in the world!" she exclaimed. Hassan laughed and held her close.

"I'm glad you like the idea. It's been a while."

"I love it. Thank you for remembering this. What did you bring us to eat, baby?"

"Ms. Minnie's fried chicken and biscuits, plus greens and macaroni and cheese from Aunt Natalie."

Everly kissed his face. "Perfect." She sat down and opened the basket, pulling out food and serving them both. Hassan pulled two beers from a side compartment lined with ice packs and opened one for his wife. The two them prayed over their food and started eating, watching the still lake and the night sky as they talked quietly.

"I have something for you," Everly said, gathering their trash. They would take the dishes home and wash them and drop the trash in one of Nate's cans when they passed his property. Hassan helped her, and once everything was put aside, they snuggled together on the blanket. Everly pulled something from the pocket of her pants and handed it to him. It was a small envelope. Hassan took it from her, nervous. Everly moved so he could use two hands. He removed four ultrasound photos from the envelope. His breath caught, and he swallowed. He felt an intense, almost bone deep sadness as he looked at the photos. His children.

"Ev, I didn't know you were holding on to these," he whispered.

"I've been having some virtual sessions with the therapist Dr. Barnett recommended," Everly said, holding his arm, "We discussed whether I needed to keep holding on to them. But then, it occurred to me that I could give them to you. You've been a rock, Hassan. Brave, strong, unfailing, and unwavering. You've held me up, and I realized you've been so busy doing it, you probably never had the chance to mourn our children yourself. You caught me when I was falling, so many times, baby. But you haven't had the moment you need to feel your feelings, whatever they are. You deserve the space to grieve what we lost, too. And you're so focused on me, I'm afraid you haven't had it. So, I'm giving these to you. They were your children too."

Hassan's hand shook as he held the photos. Tears blurred his vision and fell down his cheeks, and suddenly he was sobbing, his shoulders shaking, his sadness and disappointment heavy. Everly pulled him against her breast, rubbed his hair, whispered words of love. He wrapped his arms around her and cried—for the chances at fatherhood he lost before he even got the chance to admit he wanted them.

"I didn't want you to see me break down and think it was your fault," Hassan admitted, sniffling. Everly kissed his forehead.

"I know, baby. I know why you held back. But you don't need to anymore. If we're really getting back to us, back to basics, you can't hide from me. We're not 'us' if we're not being honest." She rubbed his head and neck, kissed him over and over. Hassan sighed.

"I really wanted those babies, Ev," he confessed. He heard Everly whimper, felt her tears on his head.

"I really wanted them too," she whispered, and the two of them cried together.

February 14th
Everly

Everly wrapped flowers, picked flowers, made arrangements, potted and repotted. Her line was out the door, and there were people milling about, pulling flowers from her refrigerated case and staying to buy other things. Freddie had been in and out all day, delivering bouquets, stuffed animals, gift baskets, and even succulents and bonsai trees. She was partnering with _Luna Sweets_, the town bakery, to add orders of chocolates and cookies to the flowers, so someone from there had been in and out all day as well.

Her husband was at his shop, cutting head after head, making sure people looked good for their Valentine's Day dates. Also, it was Friday, and people loved to get fly for the weekend, no matter what they were doing. Both of their businesses ensured they'd have no time to think of their own plans for the day until they were closing. But Everly wasn't fazed, because she only had one plan for today: strip her husband naked and ride him until she fell asleep.

It had been more than six weeks since she felt Hassan inside of her, and while she loved his romantic rebuilding, she missed the physical intimacy that usually accompanied her husband's attention. Everly knew Hassan was giving her time to come to him, to feel comfortable, and after their night picnic, she was. She hadn't seen her husband so vulnerable in years, and it reminded her how connected they were. And she realized there was an important piece of their connection she was still missing. Tonight, she was going to get it.

Everly and Hassan had always had a strong physical attraction. She wasn't one of those people who believed it was separate from their romantic makeup, or less important to their union than other things. She loved her husband's touch; more than that, she loved seeing his response to *her* touch, and she loved when they reached the pinnacle of passion together. Making love was as necessary as making conversation, and she hoped her and Hassan would make it until they weren't able to anymore... starting with tonight.

"Ev, were you able to—"

"Nate, your order is on my worktable in the back," she interrupted him as he bypassed the line and walked up to the counter, "And you're lucky. You got the last twelve. I'm about to send Freddie to my greenhouse again." Nate had called the night before frantic, asking her to please set aside a dozen pink roses for Sassy.

Everly guessed he was ready for them to make up, and she was happy. Sassy was good for him, she needed someone like Nate, and Nate's attitude had been horrible while they weren't speaking. Nate breathed a sigh of relief and went to the back, getting his boxes and jetting back out the door. Other patrons looked at him as he passed, some with stank faces because he was able to skip the line. *Oh well*, Everly thought with a shrug, *I'm gonna hook my family up every time.*

She continued ringing people out and handing off prepaid orders. She was fast, and her flowers were flawless. Hassan always asked why she never brought on extra help for the big flower days—Valentine's Day, Mother's Day, Memorial Day, but Everly liked the hustle and bustle. She liked the way the time passed when she was busy.

"Ms. Everly, do you have any more of these?" a woman called to her, holding up the last pre-made bouquet of white calla lilies and red roses.

"Not premade, but if you don't mind waiting while I check these people out, I'll do you up a fresh one," she called back. The woman grinned, nodding her head. Everly smiled back and nodded to a seat on the side, inviting the woman to sit.

"Okay, on my way to the greenhouse. I'll back in about thirty minutes," Freddie said, his hand grasping the list she'd given him. Everly nodded.

"Good. I already texted my brother and sister-in-law. Tiara will make sure you get everything on the list, and MJ will help you load," she said. Her older brother had been a career soldier, and after twenty-five years, was enjoying his retirement from the military. Tiara did medical billing, but she worked from home; neither one of them had any problems helping her out. Everly always said a prayer of thanks for her supportive family. Freddie left quickly, and Everly finished her checkouts.

The line died down, and the store just had a few people browsing, so Everly got her materials from the back and whipped up another rose/ calla lily arrangement for her patient customer. The woman left smiling, her arms full of beautiful blooms. Everly sighed. Making people happy was her favorite part.

Hours later, the shop was finally empty. Everly sat behind the counter, drained. She contemplated staying closed the next day. The idea was more appealing the more she thought about it.

"It's not like I have anything to sell," she mumbled to herself. She could sleep late, and spend the day in the greenhouse, gathering flowers to restock.

"Look at my fine ass Foxglove. You're worn out, aren't you, baby?" Hassan came through the door, a teasing smile on his face.

Everly giggled. "You really have been studying your flowers lately. I don't think you've ever called me a Foxglove, either."

"I gotta keep you on your toes," he bragged, dusting off his jacket. He came around the counter and pulled her into his arms. His hands went to the small of her back and applied gentle pressure, massaging where he knew she was sore from standing all day. Everly looked into his eyes, saw her past, present, and future. She'd never felt safer.

"Your hands feel amazing, baby," she whispered, maintaining eye contact, letting him see her desire. He responded in kind, holding her tighter. She could feel his heart beating faster, and Everly smiled, her confidence soaring, knowing this man was affected this way by her and *only her.*

"I was going to suggest the drive-in, but I'd probably fall asleep on the movie. I called Fresh Catch and got their last dinner reservation. We can go—"

"It's been a long day, husband. Let's go home. I am certain we have something in the fridge I can turn into dinner. MJ and Tiara are at the drive-in with everyone else, and the kids are up at the main house with PawPaw. We'll be totally alone. I wanna kiss and cuddle with you."

"Anything you want, my wife," Hassan whispered and gave her a gentle kiss. He helped her clean up and agreed she should stay closed Saturday and work on restock. They left the store and got on the road home. Pulling up to their house, Everly was filled with a sense of excitement and pleasure. She was going to be alone with her husband, free to touch and kiss him as she pleased, free to rediscover him the way she'd been hesitant to for weeks.

Inside the house, Hassan lit the fireplace while Everly searched their kitchen for a dinner option. Since her husband had originally planned for seafood, she pulled some shrimp and scallops, butter, wine, and lemon. They were out of pasta, but they did have rice, so Everly got everything ready. She started the meal while Hassan took a shower, and he finished it while she took hers. Then they sat down to dinner by candlelight.

"This is good, baby," Hassan said, with his mouth full. Everly nodded in agreement.

"It is. And it's pretty much what you would have ordered anyway."

"You know me so well," he chuckled. The meal was mostly quiet, but comfortable. Hassan kept their glasses filled, and ease settled over them. After dinner, the husband loaded the dishwasher and Everly went to their bedroom with two more drinks for them. She changed into a nightgown and got into bed, setting up their mountain of pillows so they could sit up against them. Then, she turned on the TV.

"Ev, do you need anything... else?" Hassan said, speaking as he came into the room and stopped short when he saw her. His eyes went wide with appreciation and lust. She patted the empty space beside her.

Everly smiled. "All I need is you, husband. Come to bed." Hassan nodded and took off his joggers and t-shirt, climbing into their big bed in only his briefs. He pulled her close, kissed her lips.

"Happy Valentine's Day," he whispered. Everly snuggled into him, lifting her face for more of his kisses. Soon, their lips and tongues smacked loudly as they tasted each other's mouths, getting lost in the feel of each other again. Hassan moved down, kissing her cheeks and neck, sucking the skin between his teeth, marking her. Everly didn't even stop him. It'd been so long; she wanted to be branded with his love.

"Yes, yes," she whispered urgently, rubbing his ears and neck. Her hands moved over his shoulders, massaging him. She was wet between her thighs and her nipples tightened. She wanted to be in his skin.

"Everly Meadows, I've missed you," Hassan growled, kissing the top of her breasts. He tugged the nightgown over her head, a lusty grin coming over his face as he looked at her naked breasts. He swooped down, his tongue circling her nipple before sucking it between his lips. Everly arched, pleasure crackling over her like a fireworks show. Her husband's mouth. *Her husband's mouth.* Lord, she'd missed it.

"Hass—baby, please—don't—"

"I won't stop, baby," Hassan finished her sentence, still giving her nipples licks and tiny bites, "I promise I'll never stop." She whimpered every time his mouth touched her, her thighs parting on instinct. Everly lifted her hips, wanting contact, needing touches. Hassan chuckled and sucked her breasts, one nipple after the other, until they were stiff and sensitive. He finally moved lower, kissing her belly, nipping at the dip of her waist, palming her thighs and spreading them wider. He gave her a positively lecherous grin and dove in, licking her slit. Everly moaned, and it turned into a startled cry when Hassan sucked her clit into his mouth. He settled in, lifting her legs onto his shoulders and palming her nipples. He ate her ravenously, mumbling how good she tasted and how much he missed her. He was a glutton, gobbling her pussy like they were sitting at the dinner table, and all Everly could do was cry and moan and scream as she came over his mouth twice.

Hassan tugged on her nipples as he tasted her and Everly was sure she couldn't take anymore.

"Hassssssss," she begged, her eyes crossing as she came again. The room was spinning. Her husband let her legs down gently, and looked up, smiling. He sat up completely and pulled his briefs off. Everly sat up, pushing braids out of her face and catching her breath. Hassan grabbed his dick and jerked it in his hand, a low groan escaping as he stared at her wet pussy. Everly whimpered and crawled to him, licking the head of his dick and pushing his hand away to suck him into her mouth. He grabbed her braids, cursing loudly as he lifted his hips and pushed deeper into her throat. Everly gagged, breathing through her nose and relaxing her throat to take his impressive length. His thickness stretched her jaws, and she moaned, loving the feeling of him in her mouth. She sucked him as eagerly as he ate her, and her pussy got wetter.

Hassan moved her mouth away, "Get on me... now." Everly obeyed his order, straddling his hips and sinking down on him. She was almost unprepared for the way he filled her, gentle but still dominant, conforming to her but still reminding her where she belonged, and who she belonged to.

"I love you, love you, love you," she sang, riding him with slow rolls of her hips and hard bounces. Hassan moaned, held her ass in his hands, looked into her eyes.

"I love you too, baby. Always and forever." The moved together, skin slapping, hearts pounding, moans and cries blending. Everly was gone, in the clouds, unable to do anything but feel. She was addicted to his love, his hard dick pressing inside, his hands and mouth on her.

"Baby, I'm coming," she sobbed, riding faster and harder. Hassan slapped her ass.

"Come on, love. Give me what I want," he growled. He lifted his hips, sliding into her more firmly and Everly exploded, her scream bouncing off the walls of their bedroom. Her entire body shook, and she cried tears of relief and pleasure. Hassan yelled her name and gathered her in his arms, lifting her off his dick as his nut splattered his thighs and stomach. They caught their breaths together and then Hassan took them into the bathroom to shower.

Later, they lay in the dark, clean and on new sheets, naked and holding each other.

"Why did you pull out?" Everly wondered.

Hassan sighed. "Because you're not on anything, and I don't want you to think or be worried about babies until you're ready again. Until *we're* ready again."

Everly nodded. Her husband was still standing in the gaps for her, still putting her first, second, and third. She could feel new leaves of hope sprouting in her heart, and she knew no matter which way they became parents, or whether they came became parents at all, he'd be by her side.

"Happy Valentine's Day, my husband," Everly whispered. Hassan's gentle snores were her response, and she laughed softly as she snuggled closer to him.

Book Bae

Lilah Meadows is a member of one of the town's founding families, and the shy, nerdy owner of the only bookstore in Luna Lake. She lost her first love a decade before, and has been hiding herself ever since, but she's ready to get swept away for the first time in a long time when she meets Aislin Kendall-Ross, avid reader and the new music teacher/ band director at Luna Lake High School.

Aislin is in Luna Lake licking her wounds after losing her job for getting involved with her co-worker, so she's wary of everyone, even the welcoming people of Luna Lake. But the beautiful bookstore owner with the kind eyes might get her to trust again.

Content Warning: Mentions of past deaths of loved ones

Color Connection

J *January 13th*
   Aislin

"As you can tell, there's some work to be done," Principal Dr. Ramona Hobbs said as they stood in the doorway of the music room, listening to the band practice. Aislin Kendall-Ross raised an eyebrow and schooled her expression before the disbelief parked itself on her face and stayed there. *Some* work? None of the sections were playing in the same key, their tempo was off, and she was sure a couple of the kids in the back were only pretending to play. *Some* work? Small town people really were optimistic, it seemed.

Aislin was in Luna Lake, NC, as the new music teacher and band director at Luna Lake High School. A musical prodigy, who played three instruments and thought one day she'd have her own school, Aislin loved creating joy through melodies and she loved children. It would seem she was perfect for this job. It didn't hurt that said job was five hours away from her broken heart, dented career, and the dumpster fire her life had become in Alexandria. Principal Hobbs had given her a much needed second chance, but she wasn't here to make friends. She was here to lick her wounds, and fade into the background. Aislin had no expectations this would be an overwhelmingly happy experience; she was aiming for adequately enjoyable, or at most, mildly pleasant. Truth be told, she couldn't relate to Principal Hobbs' optimism at all. Aislin was out of optimism; she hoped being pragmatic and polite would be enough.

"Y-yes, I can see we have some hills to climb. But not to worry, Principal Hobbs, I am the right person for the job," she said, hoping to convince the other woman and herself.

The principal smiled warmly. "I know you still have to get to know us, but we're not so formal here in Luna. Most of the staff and students call me Dr. Mona. You can too."

"Thank you, Dr. Mona," Aislin replied, a little surprised and a little more at ease, "Like I was saying, I won't let you down. I know I can make a difference. This job is—"

"Aislin, you don't need to continue selling yourself, dear. We've already hired you," Dr. Mona said with a wink and a smile, "I have no doubt you'll whip our little Loggerheads into shape."

"Loggerheads?" Aislin asked, confused.

Dr. Mona grinned. "We're the Luna Lake Loggerheads, named after the sea turtles common to the coastal plains of our great state. The children aren't always thrilled to be called sea turtles, but loggerheads are tough, and adaptable, and they endure despite threats to their way of life. A comparison to them is an honor, in my book."

"Then I'm honored to be a Loggerhead too," Aislin said, smiling back. The awful music finally stopped and the woman in front of the room directing, sat down as though she was tired. Aislin understood. It had to be a challenge directing three sections when none of them were doing the same thing at the same time.

"You sounded much improved, my dears," Dr. Mona said, moving into the room with Aislin trailing her, "I love your commitment. Let me introduce you to Ms. Aislin Kendall-Ross, your new band director and music teacher. Ms. Ross, this is your high school band, and Ms. Willis, our substitute music teacher."

"Hello, everyone. It's wonderful to be here, and I hope we'll work well together," Aislin said, waving at everyone in the room. The children's eyes filled with interest, and Aislin knew it was because she didn't look like any music teacher they'd ever seen. Ms. Willis stepped forward, her lip curled up, and her eyes filled with suspicion.

"Welcome to Luna Lake, Ms. Ross," she said, offering her hand. Aislin took it, smiling. She could already tell Ms. Willis didn't like her, but as long as she kept it cute and her mouth didn't run away with her, they'd be fine. *Maybe she was supposed to get this job permanently*, Aislin thought, remembering the "substitute" title. Either way, it wasn't her beef. She didn't hire *herself*.

"Ms. Willis, why don't you come with me? Band practice has another twenty minutes, and Ms. Ross can use it to get to know the children," Dr. Mona said smoothly, and left the room. Ms. Willis followed, sighing dramatically. Aislin smirked. Then she moved to the front of the room and looked out over the rows of chairs in a semicircle.

"Let's get the hard stuff out of the way. My name is Aislin Kendall-Ross. You can call me Ms. A, or Ms. Ross. I am from Alexandria, Virginia. I was a musical prodigy, meaning by the age of ten, I could play three instruments at the professional level—piano, bass guitar, and the violin. I am also passable on the clarinet. Yes, my hair is pink and purple, no it's not a wig or a rinse, and it's this color because they were my mom's favorites. Yes, the nose ring and tattoos are real, and no, I won't take it out or cover them up—I like myself, and I don't hide myself. And yes, I've told Dr. Mona all of this, and she hired me anyway." When she was done, the kids laughed, as she'd hoped, and the ice was broken.

"Now, I want to know about you. And I don't mean simply your names. I want you to tell me your name, what you'd like me to call you if it's something other than your name, your grade, and why you chose the instrument you're playing now." After she finished her request, Aislin started with the first row, gestured at the kids to begin their introductions. It went quickly, and she grabbed a pen and pad and made a note of anyone who had a nickname or preferred name.

"My name is Matthew Hobbs III. I'm a sophomore. Um, you can call me Ox. Dr. Mona is my grandma, and I play this clarinet because she makes me," a solidly built, medium brown boy at the end of the second row stated. The kids laughed and Aislin coughed a little, swallowing her laughter too.

"I see. Lovely to meet you, Ox. Your grandmother *makes* you play the clarinet?"

"Nah, she just made me join the band. I play a lot of basketball, and she said I needed to be well-rounded. By the time we were picking electives, it was either this or Astronomy Club, and it ain't no girls over there," Ox replied.

Aislin did laugh this time. "An honest man—I can respect it. Why'd you choose the clarinet?"

"It seemed easy, but I ain't gon lie, Ms. A—it ain't easy at all."

"The clarinet is actually a favorite for beginner musicians and *is* easier compared to other woodwind instruments. It would also be easier if you practiced, Ox, but I'll bet with your basketball schedule and you only doing this for your grandmother, you don't practice, do you?"

Ox shifted his weight, dropping his eyes. "No ma'am," he mumbled.

"Chin up. I told you I like honesty. You know why? Because when you're honest, I know when something's wrong and I can fix it. I can't fix a problem I don't know is happening. And there's no bigger problem in a band than being paired with the wrong instrument. Now, it's a new term, which means there could be some room to switch electives if you want to walk away now. We can also either pair you with something else or recommit to the clarinet. If you pick the last one, I can show you how ten minutes a night will make you better in two weeks. Do you want to walk away, Ox?"

Ox smiled, his eyes lighting up, "No ma'am, Ms. A, I want to stay. And I want to keep the clarinet."

Aislin grinned. "I love your committment. We're gonna have you so prepared you'll be able to give Dr. Mona her own concert at your family dinner. Okay, who's next? Introduce yourself, please."

Aislin was with the band longer than the twenty minutes of practice there was left, but she didn't mind. She loved meeting the kids and figuring out why they were in the band. As it turned out, many of them were embarrassed by the band playing so poorly, but the former music teacher had no real musical experience, neither did Ms. Willis, and their parents and other adults cheered the same whether they played well or not, so the kids went along with it. Aislin was impressed with their tenacity; she'd been at schools where the kids and parents would have given up by now. She was confident she could help and was suddenly feeling like her adequately enjoyable stay in Luna Lake might even pass mildly pleasant and go further. She might even be... content, one day.

Aislin drove around after she left the high school, trying to get a feel for the town. There were still lingering decorations from Christmas, and it gave Main Street a wonderful glow. Twinkling lights in the trees and on the lamp posts made it feel bright, even in the nighttime. She passed the library, a flower shop called *Luna in Bloom*, with a wonderful garden display in the front window, and several closed businesses. Then she saw it. A bright white building, with an awning of alternating pink and purple stripes. The colors called Aislin, made her pull over and park her car. She got out and approached the door, which was lit by two bright sconces and flanked by a display window on each side. Underneath the windows were pink plant boxes filled with purple pansies and winter daphnes. Pink and purple, followed by pink and purple. Aislin looked up at the sky.

"What are you trying to tell me, Mama?" she whispered. She focused on the sign above the door, and the shelves she could see inside. *The Neverending TBR*. It was a bookstore. Aislin's gaze flitted to the two windows, finally noticing one was dressed with a tower of books shaped like a Christmas tree, with lighting all through it, and the other like a private reading nook with a chair, blanket, small table, lamp and a pile of books. Aislin smiled. She'd had to sell what she could of her book collection, and abandon the rest, only able to bring her very favorites to Luna Lake for her new start. Clearly, this was her mother's way of telling her to start new in other ways too. She pulled on the door and went inside.

The interior was cozy, done in a colorful, boho style with soft, mauve, walls and pendant lighting in the shape of flowers, hanging from the ceiling. There were light wood bookshelves wall to wall, from the front to the back, and round tables full of books interspersed throughout. The hardwood floors looked worn, but in a way that meant the store saw a lot of customers, and each table had a pink and purple paisley patterned rug underneath it. There was a small lavender sofa and light-colored wood coffee table separating the front and back halves of the store, and strategically placed mint green club chairs for reading. In the back left corner, there was a staircase, and a sign at the bottom, "Cafe Upstairs." The checkout counter was in front, off to the right, and one of the finest women Aislin had ever seen was sitting behind it.

She was very round, and her light skin looked slightly flushed. Her lovely breasts pushed out of the V-neck top of the shirt she was wearing, and the headband tied around her auburn hair held the same pattern as the shirt. She was wearing big, square-framed glasses and reading a book. Aislin was stuck. The woman's full bottom lip was between her teeth as she immersed herself in the novel, and her pert nose was scrunched in concentration. Aislin couldn't see her eyes yet, but she'd bet money they were beautiful. The world spun a little faster, and everything she'd told herself about never getting involved again, felt like it was going out the window.

"Welcome to *The Neverending TBR*," the woman said, using a bookmark to hold her place, and finally looking up. Aislin licked her lips, her response sticking in her throat. As she suspected, the woman's eyes were beautiful. Slightly slanted in shape, and the color of dark terra-cotta, shifting shades between browns and oranges as the light hit them. Aislin was damn near speechless. And she wanted to touch her.

Lilah

Lilah Jean Meadows yawned and rolled her shoulders. It had been a busy day at the store, and for once she regretted opting to stay open later than most other places on Main Street. She tapped her cell phone screen to wake it up and look at the time. Thirty minutes, and she could shut this down for the day. At least there wouldn't be much to do. The cafe closed an hour earlier than the store, so it was already clear up there, and she'd cleaned up. The bell dinged, and someone came through the door. Lilah didn't glance up right away; she was reading *Sinful Desire*, finding out Cian O'Sullivan had been building Gianna Bianchi a house before they were even together, and she was riveted. *That's the kind of ro-*

mance and intention I need in my *life*, she sighed. She stuck a book-mark in to hold her place.

"Welcome to *The Neverending TBR*," Lilah said, and looked up. Her eyes widened, and her mouth was suddenly dry. The woman standing in front of her was gorgeous. She looked taller than average, maybe about five-foot-eight, and her skin was the color of Mississippi red clay, rich with oranges and browns, against a ruby backdrop. Her hair was a mass of curls alternating pinks and purples and it moved as she did. She had a gold ring in her wide nose, and the biggest, darkest, eyes Lilah had ever seen. Her body wasn't completely visible because she was wearing a jacket, but her ink peeked from her wrists and her neck. Her thighs were thick in her distressed jeans and her hips looked wide. Lilah wanted to touch her. *Calm down*, she berated herself, *it's been awhile, but there's no need to scare her.*

"H-hello. I-I just—I wanted to check—I'm new here, and I thought I'd check out your store," the woman stammered, but finally got her sentence out, those full, juicy, lips trembling like she was nervous. Lilah smiled a little, her cheeks warming. She hadn't made anyone nervous in a long time.

"Of course. Make yourself at home. I'm closing in half an hour, but you can check us out to your heart's content until then. I'm Lilah," she introduced herself, trying to hide that the woman made her nervous too.

"I'm Aislin. Nice to meet you, Lilah," the woman said back, her slightly husky voice making Lilah shiver a little. She walked past the counter and deeper into the store, her small smile growing. Aislin headed right to the nonfiction section, perusing until she found music books. *A musician*, Lilah thought. From her book choices, along with the hair and nose ring she'd heard about from everyone who stopped in the store that afternoon, she surmised

Aislin must be the new teacher and band director at the high school.

"It's beautiful in here," Aislin called out, running her hand over the book spines, as if she were mesmerized. Lilah understood. She got lost in here herself most days.

"Thank you. This place is my pride and joy, my solace. It saved me after... anyway, the store is everything to me," she replied, swallowing her words about why the store was so important. Her heart clenched. Elle's face drifted into her mind. She'd thought her life was over after she lost Elle. This store had given her something to hold onto, something to live for. Aislin peered over, as if she wanted to ask what was wrong, but stayed silent. Then she gave Lilah another small smile and went back to studying the bookshelves. Lilah picked up her book again.

Fifteen minutes later, Aislin sat a huge stack of books on the counter in front of her, smiling wide. Lilah laughed; her obvious joy was infectious.

"Think you got enough?" she teased, starting to scan them. Aislin shrugged.

"I've got enough to start. I lost most of my library when I moved; I love to read, and I'm looking forward to building it back up."

"It's a good thing you found me, then."

"Yeah, it is. You've got a great selection. I wondered whether I'd have to go to Wilmington, but I'm pretty sure you have everything I need."

"If I don't, I can get it," Lilah said, grabbing one of her large, printed tote bags. She smiled over at Aislin, feeling warm. A beautiful, musical, woman who loved to read, and whose hair matched her store? That kind of kismet was unheard of, and Lilah didn't know where it would lead, but she didn't intend to let it pass her by. She bagged the books, and swiped Aislin's card for the total, handing it back along with a receipt.

"You gonna be okay here, closing by yourself?" Aislin suddenly asked, slinging the strap of the tote bag over her shoulder.

Lilah smiled. "Yes, thank you. I'll be fine. Don't worry about me; make sure you get those books home, and don't stay up too late reading. You have school tomorrow."

"I—how did you—"

"Word travels fast in a small town, and look at you, Aislin—nose ring, tattoos, big purple hair. The old folks are in a tizzy. But mostly, everyone's all aflutter, thinking the band might actually be good one day."

Aislin laughed. "The band will be fine—they just need a bit of focus, and bit of practice. I'll do my best not to let the town down."

"You won't; I've got a good feeling about you, Aislin," Lilah said, sounding flirty even to herself. *Where the hell did that come from?*

"I'll take your word for it, Lilah. You have a good night," she said back, turning to leave. With one last wave, she was gone, and Lilah blew out a deep breath, flustered and warm. The new music teacher had her acting out of character with one interaction. *Let me close this store,* she thought, shutting down her POS system after totaling her transactions for the day. *Clearly, I need to go home and have a date with my rose if one pink/ purple-haired woman has me behaving this way.*

But thoughts of Aislin would not be so easily dismissed. Lilah thought about her on the drive to her grandfather's house to check on him, on the subsequent drive to her own house, and all through her makeshift dinner of leftover fried rice, half of a pork chop sandwich, and sweet potato pie. Lilah continued to think of Aislin while she relaxed in the tub, and in bed while her fingers rubbed her swollen, sensitive, clit until she whimpered her release and fell into a dreamy sleep.

The next day, Lilah Meadows woke up relaxed, and refreshed, but also confused. No one had ever stayed on her mind so long after first meeting them. Not since Elle, anyway. What did it mean?

"You don't even know if she likes girls, Lilah," she mumbled to herself as she scrambled some eggs, "It would be just your luck if the first woman to turn your head in years turns out to be straight." But something told her Aislin could feel their attraction, and that she received it, and reciprocated it.

An hour later, Lilah was unlocking the door to her store. She dropped her coat and tote bag behind the counter and hit the lights, making sure to turn on her book tree and the twinkling lights in her window. She knew it was time to take her holiday decorations down, but it was so festive, and she loved how it made her feel. Lilah went upstairs to the cafe, turned on the POS system, and put the daily allotment of cash in the drawer. Then she started the coffee machines and the hot water for tea, checked stock on tea bags, sugar, substitutes, and creamers and went back downstairs. In thirty minutes, someone from *Luna Sweets*, the town bakery, would bring her daily order of treats she sold alongside the drinks. This week, she'd ordered individual sized cranberry cobblers, sweet potato pie, decorated sugar cookies, lemon bars, and chocolate covered biscotti.

The cafe above the store had been a dream of Elle's, one of many she had years ago, when she and Lilah were going to open the store together. Lilah was skeptical of it, but after Elle died, she vowed to keep it in the design, and make it work, no matter what she had to do. It would be her tribute to her love. And it turned out to be a such a hit, Lilah wished Elle was there to say, "I told you so."

Thoughts of Elle took her back down to the main level, where she sat behind the counter and waited for her staff. She had two employees who ran the cafe for her while she stayed below and sold books. As she waited, Lilah looked around, thinking of her one and only love.

Lilah met Elle Tanner when she was a junior in college. The two of them hit it off immediately, and for the next ten years, loved, lived and dreamed together. It was everything Lilah ever wanted and more. She brought Elle back to Luna Lake with her, and they took jobs in Wilmington. Elle didn't mind living in a small town; she thought it was cool Lilah had so much legacy and history in one place.

When they were thirty, the two of them, who were both working in publishing, decided to open their own bookstore. Lilah was looking forward to a lifetime of love and books, but it wasn't to be. Elle's autoimmune condition proved to be too much for the medication she was using to regulate it, and one day, she collapsed in their home. A month in the hospital, with Lilah at her side, watching her lose the battle with her own body. She died just weeks after Grandma Bizzy, and for a while, Lilah was convinced the grief would consume her, and she'd die too. But she made it through, and a decade later, her and Elle's dream was still a reality.

The door opened and Lilah looked up, smiling at her two employees, Frankie and Norah, and the delivery person from *Luna Sweets* who was behind them.

"Morning, Boss," Frankie spoke first, smiling back.

"Good morning, Lilah," Norah followed.

"Good morning, you two. Your timing, as you can see, is perfect," Lilah said, and they laughed. They hung their jackets on the rack beside the door and helped with the pastries. Lilah turned on her POS system and counted the money in her cash drawer. She sent up a small prayer of thanks; she was grateful her thoughts of Elle no longer took her to a dark place. She'd always mourn, but she wanted to be happy again—and she knew Elle would want her to be happy too.

Unbidden, thoughts of Aislin drifted into Lilah's head again. Her perfect red-brown skin, her thick thighs, her beautiful hair. She was an apparition, an unforeseen disruption in the monotony, a glitch in the matrix. How she'd shaken Lilah's world so fast was a mystery, no more known than how she'd walked into her store with hair in Elle's two favorite colors, expounding on her love of books, Lilah's very first love as well.

"What are you trying to tell me, Elle?" Lilah whispered, looking up. She sighed. Maybe she was reading too much into this. *Besides,* she thought with a smile, *Aislin probably won't even have the time to entertain anything. The band needs her way more than I do.*

"You're all set, Ms. Meadows," the delivery person told her, coming back downstairs and grabbing his cart. He stuck out a clipboard and Lilah signed the paper attached, letting him go on his way. A moment later, Frankie descended the stairs with a steaming mug and two biscotti on a plate.

"First cup," he said, like he did every morning, and sat the mug and plate on the counter in front of her. Lilah smiled.

"Thanks, Frankie. You guys ready up there, or you need me?"

"We got it, Boss. Enjoy your coffee," he replied easily, going back upstairs. Lilah knew he and Norah would also have a cup of coffee and a pastry while it was still quiet. She dipped her biscotti and took a bite, appreciating the quiet time as well.

Open Books to Open Looks

J*anuary 20th*
 Lilah

"It's a national holiday, LJ. Why would you open?" Lilah's cousin Hassan asked her as they talked on the phone. Lilah was on her way to the store to open, and Hassan was taking a break on his back porch and enjoying the morning air. He'd actually called her; he was trying to get back to romance with his wife Everly and wanted her advice. They'd recently suffered a pregnancy loss and were drifting apart; Hassan was trying to get them back on track as best he could, and Lilah wanted to help her favorite cousin.

"Many people have started thinking of MLK Day as a Day of Service—a day to be on, not off. A day to be active in the community. I have two whole displays of books about him, community work, grassroots organizing, and societal change. I'll be open for anyone who wants to learn—or anyone who needs a quiet place to read."

"Luna Lake *has* a library, LJ," Hassan teased. Lilah laughed.

"A library that is observing the holiday by being closed, Hass. Don't be a smart ass."

"Okay, fine. Go to your bookstore. The shop is closed, so I'll be by to check on you." Hassan ran *Luna Cutz*, the oldest barbershop in Luna Lake. It had been in their family for seventy years, and used to be run by their grandfather, Harlan Meadows. Gramps had been in an alcoholic spiral since their grandmother passed a decade before, and Hassan took over the shop for him. He was an expert barber, the job was perfect for him, and he loved it.

"Then I'll see you later. Go make your wife breakfast in bed," Lilah instructed, pulling up to *The Neverending TBR*.

"You know, breakfast in bed isn't a bad idea. Thanks, LJ. Love you."

"Love you back." Lilah ended the call and got out of the car. Main Street was so quiet, you could hear a pin drop. It was early still, but the quiet would persist. Nothing would open today, except the hospital, police station, and the community center. She unlocked the door and went inside, turning the sign over to "Open," and hitting the light switch. The store lit up, bright and perfect, the way she'd left it the night before. Lilah dropped her tote bag and shrugged off her jacket, hanging it on the coat rack. She went behind the counter and turned on the POS system, then unpacked her bag, pulling out her travel mug full of coffee and a warm croissant. She'd brought food from home today; Lilah wasn't going to force Frankie and Norah to work on a holiday, so the cafe wouldn't be opening.

Once Lilah was settled in her chair, she pulled her book from her bag. The year before, she'd started stocking Black independent romance books in her store, and not only were they flying off the shelves, but Lilah also was addicted to them. She opened *I Wanna Be Down* by AshleyNicole. Something told her this one was going to be good.

The bell dinged and the door opened just as Sesali was admitting to her friends she'd been keeping her friendship with Dash a secret, and Lilah almost cursed whoever was coming in. Until she looked up and saw Aislin, dressed down in a sweatsuit and J's, pink and purple curls big and wild all over her head, nervous smile on her face.

"Oh, hi," Lilah said, grinning, "I wasn't expecting you today." Aislin had been coming by the store every night since the first night, browsing the shelves, reading, and talking to Lilah. Their conversations were mostly surface level, but they enjoyed each other's company.

"I didn't feel like being home alone, so I was going to take a drive. But when I got to Main Street, I noticed you were open, so I stopped in. I... wanted to see you," Aislin admitted, her smile widening. She took off and hung her jacket, then headed to the mystery shelves, perusing titles. Lilah tried to speculate how many she would leave with. Every time she came in, Aislin would buy at least three books to take home with her. Lilah wondered where she was keeping them all. She knew Dr. Mona had arranged for Aislin to rent old Ms. Meredith's guest house, behind her cottage, near the side of the lake where Nate Harper lived. It was fully renovated, cozy and private—but it was barely a studio apartment. Lilah doubted there was room for a library.

Aislin pulled two books from the shelf and settled herself on the lavender sofa.

Lilah cleared her throat. "Um, the cafe won't be opening today, and it'll probably be just me and you here, so let me know if you get hungry or thirsty and I can see what we have up there."

"I'll be fine, Lilah. Don't go out of your way for me," Aislin said. She put the books down and stood up, walking over to the counter, "Why is it you and me, today? What are you doing here?"

Lilah put her book down, and pushed her glasses up on her nose, Dash and Sesali forgotten for the moment, "I wanted to have a Day of Service, in my own way. I have books on MLK, and community work. I blasted on all of the store's socials that I would be opening for anyone who wants to learn more or needs a safe space."

"You're incredible, you know," Aislin said, and then dropped her eyes, like she was embarrassed. Lilah giggled.

"Thank you."

"You should be home with your honey, sleeping in and watching TV. And here you are instead, trying to educate the masses."

"My honey died some years ago, but this store was our brain-child; if she were alive, she'd probably be here with me," Lilah said, shrugging.

Aislin frowned. "I'm sorry, Lilah. My mouth, sometimes it—"

"You're okay, Aislin," Lilah interrupted, "How would you have known? Besides, I can handle talking about her. Elle was... amazing. She dreamt up this store with me, and I feel her every time I open the doors. You didn't do anything wrong."

"I can hear the love in your voice. I wish I'd had a love so pure," Aislin said, sighing at the end. Lilah came from around the counter and took her hand. It was warm and soft. She tugged gently and walked them both over to the couch. When they were sitting down, Lilah faced her.

"Tell me what happened. What made you sigh like you did? Who put that pain in your voice?"

Aislin shook her head. "I'm fine, and you don't want to hear about my issues. I'm a bad luck charm of the highest order, and I don't want to run away the only friend I have here."

"Do you see me running away?" Lilah questioned. She grabbed Aislin's chin, lifting her head and staring into her dark eyes, "But I know *you're* running away from something. You can tell me... you can trust me."

Aislin's eyes filled with tears, and Lilah's heart clenched. Someone hurt her. The thought made her want to fight. For the first time since Elle died, she'd met someone whose happiness she'd fight for. It was happening so fast, but Lilah knew better than to question whether it was real. She knew Elle was the one the moment they met.

"I'm sure you heard I'm a bit of a prodigy. I was touring as a classical pianist by the time I was fifteen. My mama acted as my manager, and she traveled with me. When I was thirty, she passed away. She was my biggest supporter and champion, but I didn't want the spotlight anymore without her, so I found work teaching at this exclusive music conservatory in Alexandria. Everything was fine for the first three years, maybe a little lonely, but fine. Then, I met Raven."

"You fell in love with her," Lilah said, and Aislin nodded. She grabbed Lilah's hand like it was an anchor and sighed again. Lilah's heart thumped with pride at being the person Aislin trusted with her story.

"I didn't think I could love anyone again after my mama was gone. Raven was pure magic to someone like me. It had been me and my mama on our own most of my life, and my career didn't leave a lot of room for relationships. Raven's attention was foreign, but so wonderful. She became a lifeline for me."

"How long were you involved with her?" Lilah asked. Aislin scowled.

"Three years. We were discreet at school—she was the orchestra conductor there—but outside, we were everything to each other. Then, her husband came home."

"H-husband?"

"Yeah," Aislin said bitterly, one lone tear falling from her eye, "They'd been separated—but not divorced—and he'd been working overseas. One day, he just came home, wanting to fix their marriage, and I guess Raven was passing time with me until she could get back with him. Before I could confront Raven about her lies, he found out about us. When *he* confronted Raven, she said *I* was the aggressor, and I played on her loneliness and seduced her into a relationship. He reported me to the school, and all hell broke loose."

"Oh, Aislin," Lilah whispered, her heart aching. She'd been preyed on, and lied to, and then she lost her job. What a mess.

"The school let me go, even though our entire relationship was offsite, and our business, and even though other people verified Raven was the one who chased me. The principal said the board didn't approve of me 'flaunting my lifestyle.' Apparently, knowing I'm gay isn't a problem, but an illicit lesbian love affair is a bridge too far. They told me they wouldn't block me from another job, but someone did because I couldn't get an interview anywhere in a fifty-mile radius. The guy who used to be my booking agent happens to have a sister who lives here, and she told him the high school was looking for someone. He did me one last favor and passed my name on to Dr. Mona. I applied, and she hired me."

"I'm glad you landed here with us—we take care of people here. But I'm sorry those things happened to you, Aislin. I'm really sorry."

Aislin shook her head. "I should have known it was too good to be true. No one ever loved me but my mama and I shouldn't have expected more. It was my fault."

Lilah frowned. "I don't ever want to hear you blame yourself again. You are not responsible for other people's lies. And you have the right to expect more. You deserve more. You deserve everything."

"Thank you," Aislin said, drawing in a calming breath and letting it out, "I've only been here a week, but this is probably the most welcoming place I've ever lived. I didn't have high expectations for happiness, to tell you the truth. I was hoping I'd be comfortable, maybe even content. I didn't even let myself *want* anything more."

"We're going to change your mind," Lilah promised, "Luna Lake isn't perfect, but I am positive you can be happy here. You just have to want it, Aislin. And you have to try."

"I will," Aislin agreed with a nod, "I will consider this a new lease on life, a new chance to have the future I want."

"Exactly. And if you want more proof, you're already making an impact. Do you know how many music and instrumentation books I've sold this week? You're changing the kids' minds already. So many more of them are excited about the band, and so much more confident. You're changing things for them, Aislin."

"I am?"

"Yes, you are. Your love of music shines out of you; they see it and are responding to it. And it's only been a week."

"They're wonderful children," Aislin said, her smile like a rainbow after a storm, "and they want to do well. Their energy is refreshing and honestly, they're doing as much for me as I'm doing for them."

Lilah smiled. "See? You're getting a new beginning, and it's what your mama wanted for you, trust me. I know it's what Elle wanted for me, and I try to make her proud every day." She was a little surprised at the way she'd jumped right into Aislin's life, but it felt right. Lilah was angry that duplicitous people had made Aislin feel like she wasn't meant for happiness or love. She remembered when Elle and her Grandma Bizzy died, and she felt the same way. But the people around her comforted and spoke life into her until she could do it for herself again. Lilah was happy to pay it forward and do something similar for Aislin.

"Thank you, Lilah. Thank you for opening your store today. It was exactly what I needed," Aislin said, grabbing Lilah's hand and kissing her palm gently. Lilah gasped softly, the feel of her lips sending tiny frissons of desire through her. Her cheeks warmed and she knew they were red.

"It was what I needed too," she whispered, and Aislin's face lit up with her smile.

<u>January 27th</u>
<u>Aislin</u>

"You don't think it's too soon to ask her out? I mean, we've only known each other two weeks."

"And for two weeks you've seen and spoken to each other every day. Your Luna Lake travel pattern is a perfect triangle from your home, to here, to her bookstore, and home again. Aislin, please."

"I've been to the diner, the hair salon, and the soul food restaurant too," Aislin mumbled. She and Dr. Mona were eating lunch in her office. She'd grown closer to the principal as she settled into her new role, and Aislin was grateful for the connection. Spending so many years on tour as a child prodigy among adults, with her mother as her closest confidant, meant Aislin was used to having older people as friends. Dr. Mona was funny, smart, and she loved her work, so it was an easy bond. Aislin had lunch with her every day, except for the days Dr. Mona left the campus to eat with her husband, Matthew Hobbs, Sr. When she ate at school, he brought her lunch from *Luna Lakeside Diner*, and he started picking up Aislin's order too. The students had turned her on to Ms. Minnie's Lakeside Special, and Aislin realized it was possible to fall in love with a sandwich; she'd had one every other day since she arrived in Luna Lake.

"My point is," Dr. Mona said, pointing a French fry at her, "You've done nothing but eat, sleep, teach music, and talk to Lilah. It's not too soon. She's all you think about."

"I think about other things," Aislin protested, though it was a lie.

"Aislin, lie again. You're buying books every day like we don't have a perfectly good library at this school, and in this town."

"Fine. She's all I think about. But... I don't want to scare her, Dr. Mona," Aislin admitted, "I haven't had a lot of lovers, or even dated a lot. I don't want to seem clingy, latching on to the first person to be kind to me. What if Lilah doesn't even think of me that way?"

"What if she does? And for the record, Lilah hasn't done a lot of dating either. Elle was her first, and only serious relationship. And Elle's been gone ten years. The two of you are more alike than you think, and both of you need this more than you realize. Besides, the worst she can do is say no."

Aislin conceded her boss was right and took a bite of her sandwich. She nodded, as she swallowed her food. It was true she was anxious to see Lilah away from the bookstore, to look into her bright eyes behind her cute glasses, hold her soft hand, watch the pink come into her light cheeks when she was excited. Aislin even started reading some of the books she'd seen Lilah read—Black independent romance novels—and she was obsessed. She hoped they could have a first date somewhere quiet, where they could talk about some of them.

"I should just do it, right? I mean, I like her a lot, and I want—I'll do it," Aislin decided, digging into her fries. Dr. Mona laughed.

"I'm proud of you, Aislin. Hiding is nice—safe, and warm—but living is so much better, darling. Your mama is pleased," Dr. Mona said with a wink. Aislin ducked her head, smiling. She felt like her mama was pleased too.

Later, at band practice, Aislin was nervous. As soon as she wrapped up here, she was going to *The Neverending TBR* to ask Lilah on a date. A date! She'd never been the most forward person, unless she was on stage, but this was bigger than a concert. This was Lilah Meadows, beautiful and kind, caring and smart. This was everything.

"Y'all ready to be brave?" she asked the band, moving to the front of the room. She'd given everyone a ten-minute break, and the students were talking quietly.

"What do you mean, Ms. A?" asked Trinity Hobbs, Ox's younger sister, and one of her fledgling flute players.

Aislin smiled. "Let's try playing together," she suggested. With so many of the kids at different skill levels, Aislin decided the best way to teach them was to go back to some basics. She cordoned them off into their own sections—woodwinds, brass, and percussion—and divided practice between the different groups. For two weeks, she mandated practice every day, and broke it into three-time intervals, working with one group on musicality while the other two groups worked on formations, stretching, and hand placement—then she would switch. She gave the band hand and finger techniques to practice for homework, and checked in with the parents to make sure it was being done. She also asked Dr. Mona to rearrange her regular music classes, so all the band kids were in one class together, and they could use their music period to work on breath control, and sheet music fundamentals. It was so much work, but so much fun, and the kids gave their very best, which fueled her to do the same.

The children looked skeptical, but Aislin had faith in them. "You've been working so hard, and I think it's time to see how much we've improved. Come on, everyone put the chairs back in a semicircle and let's do this." The kids put the room back into traditional rehearsal format and sat down. Aislin went to the piano and sat down as well. She ran her fingers over the keys, taking a deep breath. She never felt closer to her mother than when she was sitting at the piano.

"Follow my lead," she said and started playing the intro to "Linus and Lucy," the *Peanuts* theme song. She slowed the tempo half a step to account for the instrumentation, but the sound was the same. The band joined her, playing earnestly, and paying attention to their hands and sheet music. The sound blended, and Aislin grinned. It was beautiful. Two weeks, and she'd been able to turn them around. The band was scheduled to play at an assembly in February and then the opening day of the Luna Lake High Baseball season in March, and Aislin was sure they'd be ready. The children began to play more confidently, smiling at each other as they realized how much better they sounded.

"Oh, my goodness! You all sound wonderful!" Dr. Mona entered the room, a couple of the parents behind her. They started clapping and cheering, and Aislin laughed as she finished, and gestured for everyone to put their instruments down.

"I guess I've gone over, again. Okay guys, pack up your instruments and I'll see you tomorrow."

"Thanks, Ms. A!" the kids yelled as they packed up their instruments and dispersed. Dr. Mona stayed, telling Ox and Trinity to wait in the hallway for her. Aislin tidied up the room, righting chairs and fallen stands, making things easier for the janitor.

"I knew you were perfect for this job, Aislin. This was meant to be," Dr. Mona said.

Aislin turned. "Even knowing the mess I was in before?"

"Even then," the principal confirmed, "You're a world class musician. If they were willing to lose you over your personal life, they didn't deserve you. And as for Raven—chile, I feel sorrier for her husband than I ever will for you. You dodged a bullet."

Aislin laughed. She'd never thought of herself as being the one who'd been spared. *But I guess I was. Raven is a liar who can't even confront who she really is, and the conservatory was just supposed to be a stop gap until I figured out my next thing, anyway. Maybe they did do me a favor, after all.*

"You're right, Dr. Mona. Thank you."

"Thank you, dear. Now get out of here. You know you have somewhere to be," she joked and left the room. Aislin gathered her things and went right out behind her. She caught the bakery before it closed and bought their last two slices of caramel apple cake. Then she went to Lakeside and bought two warm ciders and headed to the bookstore.

When she got there, Lilah was checking out a small line of customers. She smiled and waved at Aislin and went back to it, while Aislin got comfortable on the couch. Once the customers were gone, Lilah came over to her.

"Hey you," she said, "Heard you had a banner day at band practice."

Aislin's brows knitted in confusion. "How did you know?"

"A couple of the parents came in after picking up their kids. They're so excited."

"We've still got some work to do. But the children are working so hard. I wanted them to hear how much better they sounded."

Lilah smiled. "It's a vast improvement, from what I've been told. Of course, Dr. Mona is already thinking of places where the band can travel and perform. Prepare yourself."

"Oh, I know. I have to slow her down at least once a day," Aislin laughed, "Come sit with me for a minute." Lilah sat down and Aislin pushed one of the cups on the coffee table closer to her.

Lilah picked it up, lifting the tab and smelling it. "You brought me cider?"

"And a slice of caramel apple cake," Aislin said, removing the container from the bag. Lilah's eyes lit up, and Aislin got lost in the brown with orange tints behind her square rimmed glasses. They were purple today, to match the purple leggings under her gray shirtdress. Her round body filled out the dress, her belly and breasts bulging, and Aislin wanted to hold her softness and never let go.

"Thank you, Aislin. How thoughtful," Lilah exclaimed and sat her cup down to open the cake. She danced a little in her seat as she broke off a piece with her fingers and popped it in her mouth.

"Lilah... can I ask you something?" Aislin said, her breathing stuttering as she focused on Lilah licking remnants of caramel from her fingers.

"Sure. What's up?"

"Would you—could we—do you wanna... go out with me some-time?" Aislin released a breath after she was finished, her body almost limp with relief. She'd done the first hard thing. Now, she had to do the second and wait for an answer. Lilah stared at her; eyes wide with pleasure. Then, she grinned.

"What in the world took you so long, Aislin? Of course, I will," she said.

"It's okay, I underst—wait, what? You will?"

Lilah giggled. "Aislin, I don't know why you'd thought I'd say no, but yes. Yes, I will."

Aislin didn't know what to do next. She hadn't planned past asking, because she hadn't wanted to get her hopes up. But Lilah said yes. She said *yes*. Aislin smiled.

"You know the town better than I do, and if you don't want to go somewhere here, I get it. We can do whatever—"

"Aislin, plan the damn date," Lilah interrupted, shaking her head, "I want to be with you, and I know you want to be with me. Plan it however you want."

"Really?"

"Yes," Lilah insisted, "Treat dating me like sitting down at the piano. No matter how long it's been, you already have what you need, and you already know what to do."

Aislin smiled. It wasn't coincidence Lilah mentioned the piano, the place where she felt most like herself, and closest to her mother. Maybe Dr. Mona was right about her being meant to be here. Lilah Jean Meadows might be the most beautiful piece she'd ever play.

Turning the Page

February 7th
Aislin

"Tell the truth: you wouldn't want to model one of your favorite characters?" Lilah asked as the two of them cooked dinner at her house. Aislin shook her head, continuing to chop tomatoes for their at-home Date Night. Lilah was asking her if she'd be willing to pose for aesthetic shots of her favorite indie romance novel, like Skylar in *We've Only Just Begun* by Nicole Falls.

"No, I'd be way too nervous. Plus, being paired up with some guy wouldn't make me feel sexy."

"What if the book was sapphic? What if we were asked to do Lennox and Noelle? Or Kiki and Charley?" Lilah said, naming two of Meka James' *Desert Rose Hookup* novellas with women love interests. She came closer, and Aislin swallowed, her desire rising. Lilah was at least four inches shorter than her, but Aislin felt nearly overpowered whenever she was close. The air was thinner, and her senses, sharper. All she could see, hear, smell—was Lilah.

"You're so beautiful," she whispered, and Lilah smiled. Aislin leaned down, pressed their lips together, and her knees went weak. Kissing Lilah was like savoring the sweetest cotton candy or sipping the smoothest bourbon—it was a high like no other. Lilah leaned up and threw her arms around Aislin's neck. She whimpered and opened her mouth; Aislin slipped her tongue inside.

She dropped the knife and turned, her hands moved to Lilah's soft, round, bottom and she rubbed it. She moaned low, her heart pounding. She was gone for Lilah Meadows and though every lick of her sense told her it was too soon, her heart didn't care. And neither did her body.

"Your kisses taste like magic," Lilah whispered, and their lips and tongues found each other again, tasting and teasing, spinning them into a vortex of passion. Aislin's nipples were hard, and her panties dampened. She pulled away, kissing Lilah's forehead.

"We should eat. You've been snacking all day—you need real food," she said.

Lilah giggled. "You don't have to keep stopping yourself, Aislin. I'm not stopping you."

"Which is why I'm stopping myself," Aislin admitted, "You're so special to me already, Lilah, and I don't want you to think loneliness is driving this. Like I'm so backed up you could be anybody. You're not just anybody."

"Gotdamn, you are so sweet to me. It makes me weak. Okay, okay, I'll stop being a horndog so we can eat."

"I didn't mean—"

Lilah cut her off with another kiss. "Stop. It was a joke." She went back to the steak resting on her board and began to cut it against the grain. Lilah's cousin Hassan, and their best friend, Nate, had dropped by earlier in the evening to grill flank steaks and corn for them. Aislin offered to do it, but Lilah insisted it was their job to spoil her outrageously and minimize her manual labor, and her job to let them. She told Aislin they took care of her car, lawn, and gutters too. Aislin was envious in two ways. She'd never had anyone take care of her so thoroughly, and *she* wanted to be the person who took care of Lilah.

"I'm ruining this, aren't I? Because I won't relax," she said, with a sigh.

Lilah shook her head. "You're not ruining anything, Aislin. Baby, all I want is to be with you. I do wish you'd relax though. You're not going to do or say the wrong thing. This is not a performance. There's no way to hit the wrong note with me, as long as you're respecting me and being yourself."

Aislin finished chopping the tomatoes and nodded. Lilah was right. She had to stop being so nervous, so worried about messing up. She was terrified of making the wrong decision, and she was taking it out on Lilah. She dumped the lettuce from the salad spinner into a large bowl and scattered the tomatoes on top. Then she went in with bacon, boiled eggs, cucumbers, grilled corn, cut off the cob, and grilled onions. Then she added blue cheese and tossed everything together.

"You ready, babe?" she asked Lilah. Lilah nodded, coming over with the board full of sliced steak. Aislin made two huge plates of salad, fanned the steak out over each, and drizzled them with dressing.

Lilah shimmied. "It looks so good, and now I'm starving."

"I'm gonna start having lunch with you so I can make sure you're eating."

"Dr. Mona would come and yell at me for stealing you, so no thank you," Lilah laughed. Aislin laughed as well, and they poured wine before moving to the alcove in the kitchen where there was a table and two chairs. After praying, they dug in, and Aislin was happy as she looked at Lilah enjoying her food. It had been her idea for them to grill something at home and then start their latest buddy read. She was glad Lilah was receptive to the idea, and even more glad they were getting along so well.

Their first date—a quiet dinner at Fresh Catch Seafood Palace—was a huge success. They talked all night about books, and reading, and their pasts. Aislin talked about her mother, about never knowing her father, about touring as a classical pianist at such a young age. She avoided talk of Raven, because there was no need to rehash it, and because she wanted to move on—fully and completely. Lilah shared the inner workings of her huge family, the loss of her Grandma Bizzy and Elle within weeks of each other, and how books saved her from expiring from grief. The conversation was so easy, and the food was delicious. After, they went to *Melodies*, Luna Lake's lounge/ jazz club to listen to music and have a nightcap. It was amazing.

After the date, they were inseparable. It had only been a week and a half, but they talked and texted constantly, and saw each other every night, even if it was only for a few minutes. Aislin was trying not to fall so damn fast, but it was *Lilah*. And Lilah was everything. She was shy and gentle, but not weak or fragile. When she spoke, it was with confidence, and you wanted to listen. She loved her work and had so much respect for books and authors. Plus, she was kind, and so loving. All those things, plus being sexy as hell, had Aislin's head spinning. Her light skin, long auburn hair, and those bright eyes drew Aislin in. Her soft, plush, body made Aislin want to touch, all the time.

"As long as we're talking about you relaxing more," Lilah said, forking a piece of steak, "I want to tell you not to overextend yourself next week. This thing with us is wonderful, but it's still new and you don't need any added pressure because it's Valentine's Day."

"Thank you for saying that baby," Aislin said, sipping her wine, "But new or not, you mean something to me and I'm not going to ignore the day."

Lilah's hiked cheeks were red as she looked down at her food. "You're so sweet, Aislin. So damn considerate and careful with me. I feel... cherished when I'm with you. And you mean something to me too."

Aislin grinned and dug into her food. It was affirming to know Lilah was falling as hard as she was.

After dinner and dessert, the two of them retired to the couch with their current buddy read, *Seeing Red* by Shon. Lilah had gotten her paperback (as well as a few others for the store) so she was excited to jump in. She preferred physical books and forbade Aislin to start without her. They both read fast, and usually didn't take longer than a day or two to finish anything, so they were perfect reading partners, yet another thing Aislin loved.

Hours passed, with the two of them leaning against each other, under blankets as a classical ensemble instrumental played in the background. Lilah heard the EP in Aislin's car on the way to their first date and expressed how much she liked it. Once Aislin admitted she was the piano player in the ensemble, Lilah bought her own copy and played it in the store every day. It was just another thing making Aislin fall harder.

"You remind me of Noah," Lilah said, turning the page. Aislin looked up from her iPad.

"I do?"

"Yeah. You're so gentle, and sweet. You never want to be a burden, and you try so hard not to be. But you don't even realize how much you bring to the people around you, how you hold them together, how necessary you are."

"Lilah," Aislin whispered in wonder, her heart pounding. Lilah leaned over to kiss her, sucking on her bottom lip. Aislin moaned, using the kiss to anchor her, because she felt like she could float away.

"Fuck, why are you so amazing?" she said. Lilah giggled.

"Born this way, I'm sure," she said, pushing off the compliment.

"If I'm Noah, you're definitely True," Aislin said, waking up her iPad again.

"You think so?" Lilah asked.

"Absolutely. True is brave, even when she's unsure, and so are you. With the losses you've suffered, a lot of people would have given up. I don't think I would have been strong enough to still open *The Neverending TBR* if the person I dreamed it up with died. You're still here, living your dream, even though it was Elle's dream too, and she can't be here."

"What a wonderful thing for you to say, Aislin. Thank you, baby," Lilah said, kissing her once more. She turned another page, and then looked up again, "I had to do it, you know? I couldn't stay stagnant, lost. I had to run into life again. I couldn't forfeit my future happiness. Elle wouldn't have wanted that for me."

"You're right—she wouldn't have. I'm proud of you," Aislin said. The two of them went back to reading, getting lost in Bliss Peak and the love Greyson, Noah, and True shared.

"Aislin?"

"Yes, honey?"

"Your mama wouldn't have wanted that for you, either," Lilah said softly, and snuggled closer. Aislin smiled.

February 14th

Lilah

"Let me get this right. You told her not to make a big deal out of Valentine's Day, so *you* could make a big deal instead?" Nate Harper asked Lilah as he helped her hang a garland of cyclamen and lilies with baby's breath around the store. She'd ordered it special from her cousin-in-law, Everly Hobbs-Meadows, the day after her first date with Aislin. The flowers were winter friendly, and they came in the right colors for her surprise. The same flowers sat in vases around the store as well. It was one big burst of pink and purple to match Aislin's hair and Lilah couldn't wait for her to see it.

"Yes, Nate. Aislin's been so worried about misstepping, about choosing wrong because the one time she gave in to her heart, the woman turned out to be a liar. She doesn't trust herself. She doesn't relax with me like I know she wants to. I want her, and we're good to each other, and I don't want her second-guessing it anymore. The wonders she's working with the band have been helping to give her some of her confidence back, and I want to help too."

"I ain't seen you this fired up about a woman in years, LJ. It's... a little nerve-wracking to see you leap so far, and so fast. I mean, this thing *is* still new. And we all thought you were in mourning."

"Elle was my first love, Nate. We built a dream together; I'm going to grieve for her for the rest of my life. But life doesn't stop, and Aislin's the first person to make me feel like I may not have to move forward alone anymore," Lilah explained.

"You were never going to be alone, baby. I'm here," Nate said. Lilah smiled.

"And I love you, but you and I both know it's not the same. If it were, you wouldn't need Sassy, would you?"

"Point taken," Nate chuckled, lifting the garland and securing it with tape, "I got you, LJ. And if you're good, I am too. Hass and I worry a lot about you though. Can't nobody take care of you like we do."

"Oh, I see. You're worried about being replaced," Lilah laughed, hopping down from the stool she was standing on, "You and Hass are so spoiled. But Aislin doesn't want to push you out of the way; there's room for everyone to take care of me."

"Which one of us did you say was spoiled?" Nate said, with a grin. Lilah winked.

"You two. But not to worry, you'll always be my best friends. Aislin will be in her own lane, like Ever is with Hass, and Sassy is with you. Besides, I know you and Hass. I'm gonna wake up one day and you'll be taking care of Aislin, just like you take care of me. You'll fall for her too."

"Too, huh? Like you did?" Nate said, finishing the garland and climbing down from the stepladder. Lilah turned away, hiding her smile. It was soon, she knew. But she couldn't help how right it felt, and she didn't want to try. Elle had taught her to trust her first instinct, to be fearless, to take what she wanted. And Lilah wanted Aislin. Nate helped her cover the windows with curtains so no one could see inside the store, and hang a wreath of the same flowers on the door.

Soon after, Nate left for his date—he and Sassy had gotten into it, but they made up and were spending Valentine's Day at the drive-in. Luna Lake Drive-In was playing Black love movies all weekend for Valentine's Day. Lilah knew half the town would be there, which is why she wasn't going. She wanted to be alone with her Aislin.

Lilah lit candles and set up a charcuterie board and wine on the coffee table. She laid gifts for Aislin on the counter, so she'd see them as soon as she came in. Aislin was coming here after band practice like she always did; Lilah told her she was closing early so they could go to the drive-in. Her girl thought it was going to be a chill, no-frills night, but Lilah had other plans.

"Honey, why did you cover the windows? I thought—Oh, Lilah," Aislin came in the door talking and then stood there, speechless. Her face was alight with happiness. She clapped her hands over her mouth. Lilah stepped forward, dressed in her favorite purple skirt and low-cut white top. Her auburn hair was loose, held back by a pink and purple silk scarf.

"Happy Valentine's Day, baby," she said. Aislin stepped forward, looking thick and delicious in an oversized purple plaid shirt, black leggings, and boots. Her dark eyes welled with tears.

"You said not to make a big deal," she whispered.

Lilah grinned. "Because it was my turn to make a big deal over you. I can't predict the future, Aislin, but this feels damn good right now and I want to hold onto it—to you. This is something to let you know I'm with you as long as you're with me."

"Lilah Meadows, I can't believe you did this."

"Open your gifts, baby," Lilah urged, nudging her toward the counter. Aislin cried as she opened the chocolate truffles, the Black romance books, and the first edition of Chopin's *Nocturnes*. Aislin held the book of sheet music to her chest, tears running down her face.

"Lilah, I can't—why would you—oh my goodness," she blubbered. Lilah laughed, wiping her own eyes. Witnessing Aislin's complete joy was unmatched. Aislin put the gifts down, and moved to her, hauling her close and kissing her. Lilah whimpered, rubbing against her, and reaching up to tug on her gorgeous hair. Their kiss was wild, frantic, heavy with lust.

"Come and sit," Lilah said breathlessly between lush kisses, "Have some wine and food with me."

"Lilah, the only thing I want to eat is you," Aislin whispered.

Lilah giggled. "Later, sweetheart. Come sit down, now." She pulled them to the sofa, and they sat. Aislin picked up a glass and took a sip before kissing her again. Then, she and Lilah fed each other small bites of meats and cheese, nuts, olives, crackers and jam. They drank wine, laughed and talked, and stared into each other's eyes.

"It looks beautiful in here. The flowers are... Lilah, this is so romantic."

"Nate helped me. He wondered if I was doing too much, but I wanted to. You're always so afraid of doing too much, too soon. I wanted to show you I feel the same way you do. If you're doing a lot, I'm doing the most," Lilah shrugged. Aislin laughed, sipping more wine.

"I love it," she said, "This is where we met, and connected, and it's perfect. You look so good, and smell so good, and I don't want to be anywhere else."

The two of them snuggled on the couch, listening to music. Snuggling led to kissing, and their kissing led to Aislin's hands going up her skirt, and into her panties. Lilah had a perfect orgasm in her arms, Aislin's thumb rubbing her clit and her mouth kissing Lilah's neck.

"Let's go," she whispered. Aislin nodded, and they cleaned up their trash, blew out the candles, gathered the gifts, hit the lights, locked the store, and left. Aislin drove them to Lilah's house, the air thick with desire and anticipation.

They were barely in the bedroom before Aislin pushed her down on the bed, reaching underneath Lilah's skirt to pull her damp underwear off.

"I'll undress you later," she promised, "I've got to taste you now." Lilah spread her legs, and Aislin went low, her head getting lost underneath the purple fabric of Lilah's skirt. A second later, she whined as Aislin's tongue licked her from top to bottom before circling her clit. The second after, Aislin was sucking on the bundle of nerves gently, making Lilah cry out and lift her hips.

"Don't run away from me, baby," Aislin whispered, "I'm just getting started." She began to lick again, her moans and slurps declaring her satisfaction. Lilah was dizzy with pleasure, her mouth open, soft cries pushing out of her involuntarily. She was soaking, almost embarrassingly wet, and Aislin licked greedily, as if she couldn't get enough. No one had ever eaten her this way.

"A—oh my God—Aislin, please—" she tried to speak in complete sentences, but it was impossible with her clit being held hostage by someone's tongue, "Fuck—I can't—oh shit!"

Lilah's orgasm hit her like a freight train, at maximum speed and power, and she could feel her release squirting out of her. Aislin kept licking, kept moaning, kept slurping. Lilah felt tears on her cheeks. She was nearly overwhelmed.

"I want more, baby," Aislin mumbled, adjusting herself and holding Lilah's thighs open, "Give me more." Lilah whimpered, lifting her hips, and her hands went into Aislin's big, curly hair. She pressed Aislin's face into her pussy, wanting to give her more, wanting to give her everything.

"Atta girl," Aislin praised and put her tongue back to work. Two orgasms later, they finally stopped long enough to get undressed. Lilah sucked on Aislin's hard nipples, rubbed her ass and between her legs. She grabbed her dildo from the nightstand and handed it to her. One of their many romance book discussions led them into talking about how they liked to make love, so Lilah knew Aislin wouldn't be surprised by what she wanted.

"Fuck me," she begged.

Aislin nodded. "Where is it?" Lilah pointed to her dresser. Aislin kissed her mouth, and got up, going to the top drawer of the dresser and removing a harness with a bullet vibrator attached. Aislin didn't care for penetration, but when she found out Lilah enjoyed it, she admitted she had experience with strapping because

Raven enjoyed it also. She grabbed the dildo and inserted it into the harness, securing it. Then she fastened it around her thighs and waist, making sure it was taut, but not hurting her. She turned on the vibrator, coated the dildo with lube, and then she and Lilah got into position. Aislin slid inside her, pushing against the bullet rubbing her clit.

"Shit!"

"Yes!"

They both cried out, and Aislin started to move. Lilah loved the fullness inside her, the sliding over her G-spot, the fabric of the harness rubbing her clit. Aislin moaned, her eyes closed as she got into a rhythm and fucked Lilah. Lilah knew the bullet was pleasuring her and seeing Aislin's ecstasy only added to hers.

"Baby, baby, don't stop," she begged. Aislin bit her lip, grunted, and moved faster. Lilah could feel another orgasm coming, her juices wetting the bed underneath her.

"Lilah—oh, Lilah—" Aislin called her name, and her hips jerked as she came, moving in short thrusts that made Lilah come too. Aislin fell on top of her, whimpering.

"I'm right here, baby. I'm right here," Lilah whispered, rubbing her back.

The two of them made love all night. Lilah licked Aislin's pussy until she begged her to stop, then they used their hands to make each other come. Aislin fucked her again—from behind this time—and they took a bath together, which led to more kissing and touching. They finally fell asleep, tangled in the sheets, smiles on their faces.

The next morning, Lilah woke to the smell of bacon. She used the bathroom, washing her face and brushing her teeth. Then she pulled a shirt over her head and went to the kitchen. Aislin was in her plaid oversized shirt from the night before and socks, flipping French Toast on the griddle.

"Good morning," Lilah said, hugging her from behind. Aislin giggled.

"It's a great morning. You hungry?"

"Yes," Lilah said. She got plates and silverware ready and poured them both a glass of juice. Soon after, they sat down to French Toast, bacon, cheese omelets, and fruit.

"I have a gift for you too," Aislin said, sipping her juice.

Lilah smiled. "Last night doesn't count?"

"Last night blew me away, Lilah. I feel like I need to buy you something more expensive now."

"You'd better not," Lilah said, cutting her French toast, "I want what you were going to give me before, because I know it's intentional and thoughtful." Aislin grinned and they continued eating.

When they were done, Aislin went to her car and came back with two gift bags. Lilah tore into them, loving presents. The bags had the same chocolate truffles she'd gotten Aislin, a bear wearing a T-shirt that said "Book Bae," and a T-shirt for her with the same words on the front and her store logo on the back. There were also new scarves for her hair, a new candle and wine glass, and an annotating kit. The last gift melted her heart. She recalled mentioning how she loved highlighting her paperbacks when she did rereads, and how she wanted to annotate more.

"Oh, Aislin, you remembered. I talked to you once about annotating, and it was like the third time you came into the store; it was weeks ago."

"I pay attention, baby," Aislin shrugged, like it was no big deal. Lilah hugged her tight, kissing her all over her face.

"And this shirt is the cutest! Can I steal this idea for the store? I've been thinking of doing something besides our tote bags."

"Of course, love. Whatever you want," Aislin said easily.

Lilah's eyes lit up. "Whatever I want?"

"Whatever you want."

"Will you be my book bae? Officially?" she asked. Aislin grinned, leaning in for a kiss.

"For as long as you want me," Aislin answered, just as their lips met.

Arrested Hearts

Officer Rick Wilkins loves his quiet life in Luna Lake, as well as the time he spends with his girlfriend Violet and her daughter Sasha, who live a stone's skip away in Wilmington. He has plans for a special Valentine's Day for BOTH his ladies--and an offer of permanence that could change their lives. But Violet's ex shows up, wanting his family again, and Rick must stake his claim.

A Strong Foundation

February 3rd
Rick Wilkins

"One of these days, we're going to arrest you for real, Mr. Harlan," Officer Rick Wilkins grumbled as he helped the drunken older man into the back of his cruiser. His partner, Officer Sabrina "Bri" Harlem, turned away and coughed to muffle the sound of her laughter. This was a weekly call for them now, and she was new enough to the police force to still find it funny. Rick was over it.

Harlan Meadows, resident drunk of Luna Lake, had been caught at the community center again, catcalling the older women of the Ladies League as they headed out after their weekly meeting. It was routine for him to show up promptly at three o'clock, grinning, whistling and blowing kisses; shaking his gin bottle in his wrinkled hand as he offered the grandmothers of Luna Lake indecent proposals until someone called the police. It was a public disturbance at best, and harassment at worst. But as a Meadows, he was a part of one of the founding families of the town; his legacy carried weight, plus everyone loved his family, and knew he was essentially harmless, so he was usually just picked up and taken home. Rick was glad this would be his last call of the day. He had moves to make. He shut the door on Harlan and got into the driver's seat. Sabrina got in on the passenger side. She picked up the radio.

"Unit 426 to dispatch. Disturbance has been neutralized. We are all clear at the community center."

"*Copy that, 426,*" dispatch answered back, and Rick started the car to head to the west end of Luna Lake.

Unlike the Hobbs' family, the Meadows didn't have a family compound. They were scattered all over town, but the original Meadows estate was still standing, a sprawling Colonial on the west side of Luna Lake, where Harlan Meadows had lived with his wife Elizabeth until she died, ten years before. "Bizzy," as she was known around town, was a gentle woman, who always had a smile on her face. Losing her sent Harlen into a spiral he'd yet to recover from, which was another reason everyone gave him so much grace. Bizzy was the light of his life, and a light in their town—it hurt them all when she passed away.

As soon as Rick pulled up at the Meadows estate, Lilah Meadows, Harlan's granddaughter, ran out the front door. Rick hopped out and opened the back door, helping Mr. Harlan out.

"Rick, I'm so sorry!" she exclaimed, her multi-colored scarf floating behind her as she hurried down the steps, "Harry was supposed to take him to get a haircut, but he was late, and Granddad tried to go by himself. I should have known he'd be harassing those poor women again."

"It's not harassment if they like it, Lilah Jean," Harlan muttered, shaking off Rick's helping hand, "Those are all my women, and they love me."

"Then why'd they call the police?" Lilah shot back, throwing her hands on her hips, "Come on in this house. I can't be fooling with you. I have a store to run." Lilah was the owner of *The Neverending TBR*, Luna Lake's sole bookstore/ cafe. It was wildly popular, both for its boho style and decor, and its gentle owner. Lilah was shy in nature, but no wilting flower; she reminded everyone of her grand-mother in that way.

"You're good, Lilah. Try to keep him supervised, okay?" Rick said, getting back into the car with a sigh. Lilah nodded. Mr. Harlan gave him the finger and Lilah slapped it down, scolding him as she helped him up the stairs and into the house. Sabrina was chuckling and shaking her head in the passenger seat. Rick started the car again, cutting his eyes at her until she stopped.

"His women? Poor Mr. Harlan," she said. Rick grunted. The situation was so ridiculous it made most other officers laugh. But Rick knew there was nothing funny about alcoholism, or grief so deep it made you run from the idea of being sober. It was sadder than anything, but everyone had been dealing with it for a decade, so Rick understood them coping with amusement.

When they got back to the station, Rick grabbed his bag and clocked out. Sabrina offered to take care of the scant paperwork on their last call, so he was clear to go. He headed to his own car and was soon on his way home. Ten minutes later, Rick pulled into the driveway of his cozy, two-bedroom bungalow. It was gray, with a black sloped roof and a little front porch. His small front lawn was perfectly manicured, even in winter, and Hosta framed the front of the house.

"Hey, Officer Wilkins!" Jade Marsh, Rick's next-door neighbor, waved to him from her front steps. Rick waved back and grabbed his bag, closing his car door and walking quickly so as not to en-courage conversation.

"You had dinner? I have some beef stew in the crockpot, honey butter cornbread's almost ready," Jade went on, smiling wide. Rick sighed. He'd told this woman he had a girlfriend more times than he could count, and she still invited him to dinner every time she saw him.

"I've got plans, thanks. Have a good evening, Jade," he said and typed in the unlock code on his front door keypad. He pushed inside and dropped his bag in the entryway. His phone buzzed as soon as he took off his jacket.

"Hey Flower Girl," Rick greeted warmly. His girlfriend, Violet Harrison, giggled the same way she always did when he used his nickname for her.

"My favorite lawman. Are you on your way?" she said back. Violet and her six-year-old daughter, Sasha, lived in Wilmington. Rick and Violet had been dating for three years.

"I just walked in. I need ten minutes to shower and change and I'll be walking back out."

"Shower over here. Sasha wants to show you her art project, and dinner's nearly ready. We miss you," Violet urged. Rick grinned. Nothing made him happier than his girls missing him and wanting him. It made his Valentine's Day surprise even sweeter.

"Alright, Flower Girl. I'll come right now, and shower when I get to you. Y'all need me to pick up anything?"

"All we need is the man who sits at the head of our table. Come on, Rick."

"On my way, love," Rick said. He checked his home quickly, then grabbed his bag and jacket and left again, getting into his car and setting the alarm via app on his phone before backing out of his driveway again.

On the fifteen-minute drive to Violet's place, Rick thought about the day they met. He'd gone to Wilmington for a law enforcement conference at the convention center and ran into her while he was exploring the nearby area for food options. Violet was on a class trip to the Railroad Museum and offered him directions to a place she loved. Rick hadn't wanted to get too flirty while her second-grade class hung on her every word, so he simply offered his number and asked her to call. Two days later, she did. And now, they were three years into the best thing in his life. Three years, and a lifetime to go.

It took six months for him to meet Sasha. At the time, she was three years old, and her father had been gone since she was one. Violet said he was irresponsible and lazy and had withdrawn from his daughter once Violet made it clear *she* no longer wanted to be with him. Rick was livid. Eschewing fatherhood because you don't have access to the mother was the worst kind of manipulation and cowardice. With that experience, he wasn't surprised Violet was wary of him meeting her daughter. But he and Sasha took to each other immediately, and he'd worked hard to prove himself and show consistency in their lives. Now, you couldn't tell Rick Sasha wasn't his daughter, and you couldn't tell her he wasn't her "Papa Rick."

Rick pulled into the lot of the apartment complex where his girls lived, parking in the open space next to Violet's gray Toyota Highlander. It was fifteen years old, dinged and dented in several places, and the back passenger window didn't power down anymore, but she loved the damn thing and wouldn't let Rick get her a new one. She said he'd done enough after he upgraded their living situation. Violet and Sasha had been living in a small apartment in a different part of town. But Rick found them a nicer place, with modern and updated decor, better security, and more amenities. When Violet balked at the higher cost, he took over the rent, wanting his girls comfortable and safe. His house was a gift from his parents, and his car was paid off years ago, so he could afford it easily and was able to shut down her protests.

Rick got his bag and got out of the car, going into the building and heading up the stairs, not bothering with the elevator since it was only three flights. He turned right at the landing and hurried to Apt. 307, using his key to get inside.

"Papa Rick!" Sasha screamed and hopped up from where she was watching TV on the couch. She ran to him and Rick dropped his bag to catch her, scooping her into his arms and hugging her tight.

"There's my baby girl," he whispered into her hair. Being a father had been one of Rick's dreams for so long. After years of loneliness and failed relationships, he was nearly ready to give up, but then he met Violet. And she loved him enough to share this sweet baby girl with him.

"You want to see my art project?" Sasha asked, smiling brightly.

"After dinner, Ladybug," Violet came from the kitchen, dish towel in hand. Rick put Sasha down and met her mother halfway, hauling her into his body and kissing her lips. Violet moaned softly, falling into his kiss, her hands gripping his shirt.

"Hey Flower Girl," Rick whispered, finally lifting his mouth from hers, "I missed you."

"Missed you more, Lawman," Violet whispered back, reaching up to wipe her lip gloss from his lip with her thumb.

"Smell good in here, girl. What you cooking?"

"We keeping it simple tonight, baby. I made some hamburger steaks, rice, gravy, and corn. Quick cheddar and scallion drop biscuits. Nothing fussy."

"I'm gonna eat the hell out of it, though. Then I'm a eat you," Rick replied with a wink, making sure to keep his voice low. Violet giggled and lifted on her toes to kiss him once more.

"Come on and sit down, Lawman. Ladybug, you want apple juice or lemonade?"

"Do we have strawberries for my lemonade, Mama?" Sasha asked, turning off the TV.

Violet frowned. "No baby, we don't. I'm sorry. I'll put it on our list."

"Then apple juice, I guess." Sasha frowned too and went to wash her hands.

"Why didn't you tell me? I would have stopped and got them," Rick said, sitting at the table in the eat-in kitchen. Violet rolled her eyes.

"She'll be fine. There are ten other drink options in this house. You can't help but to spoil her behind."

"She's my baby girl," Rick shrugged. Violet laughed and started making plates.

"Your baby girl can have apple juice tonight—she'll be okay."

Rick went to the ensuite in the primary bedroom to freshen up and then returned to his seat at the table. He watched his girlfriend portion out food for the three of them. Violet wasn't a short woman, capping out at five-foot-ten barefoot, but he eclipsed her easily at six-foot-four and she said she loved how he made her feel dainty. She was thicker than a center cut pork chop with wide hips, big titties, a nice, jiggly belly, and a fat ass. His baby had a wagon that barely behaved in her pants and was so unruly in a dress, she didn't even wear them to work anymore. Rick loved every inch of her and his hands tingled as he thought about touching her later. She turned and he smiled onto her golden bronze, heart-shaped face. Her chubby cheeks, slanted whiskey-colored eyes, and full, soft mouth made her irresistible. She kept her and Sasha's hair natural and curly, either with a twist-out or flexi-rods (both things he only knew about because she explained them).

Sasha came out of the bathroom and sat down at the table. Violet set a plate in front of her, then set one with five times more food on it in front of Rick. She quickly grabbed the plate she made for herself and sat down, bowing her head so Rick could say the blessing.

Hours later, dinner and dessert were done, and they watched a couple of shows as a family after Sasha regaled them with her art project. Baby Girl was sound asleep after a bedtime story, and Violet was in bed waiting for him. Rick was in the bathroom, brushing his teeth. His shower was long and hot, easing the tension in his shoulders and removing the day from him. It was stressful being a police officer, even in a quiet place like Luna Lake. But he was about to make a major change, and hopefully his Flower and their baby girl would take the ride with him.

"Lawman? What's taking you so long? I wanna snuggle," Violet whined. Rick chuckled. She loved being up under him, skin to skin, wrapped around him. He usually worked a 4/40 shift—four days on patrol, for ten hours a day—followed by three days off. And he always went to his girls for those three days. Violet had gotten clingier over the last year, and he knew not living together was starting to wear on her. He didn't blame her; he felt the same way.

Rick walked out of the bathroom and got into bed naked, knowing Violet was too, and the door was locked so Sasha couldn't walk in on them.

"Come here, Flower Girl, with your fine ass. How was school today?"

Violet giggled as he kissed her neck. "Same as always. But Tanya Richards' father is flirting again. I threatened to take it to the principal this time. I mean, if being my student's father, and having a wife ain't enough to slow you down, then me having a man who carries a gun should do the trick. But his ass is still playing."

"Say no more. I'll be in your classroom for dismissal tomorrow," Rick vowed. Violet shook her head.

"No, baby. We agreed I would handle this according to the school protocol. And I know you ain't worried about him."

"I'm worried about his hearing. Because you should have only had to tell him once to leave you alone. Maybe if I straighten him out myself—"

"If I can't straighten Jade out, you can't do nothing to my student's dad," Violet said.

"Flower, that's different—"

"It ain't. At this point, nothing you say is penetrating. But you won't let me have a woman-to-woman discussion with *her*. Meanwhile, she keeps violating. What did she offer to feed you tonight?"

"Beef stew and honey butter cornbread," Rick mumbled, wishing he'd never pressed the issue. Violet didn't need to make a fuss. He didn't want anyone but her.

Violet slapped his chest. "See? Every damn day! Why can't I—"

"Jade is just a little extra friendly. Now, I agree they're both crossing boundaries, but this nigga is being inappropriate in your professional environment. Persisting even though you're saying no. Compromising your position. What if the principal takes it to him and he says *you* came on to *him*?" After he finished, Violet pushed out of his arms and sat up in bed. He knew she was only contemplating his words, and he gave her space to think. He knew his Flower Girl. She'd need his arms soon enough.

Sure enough, after a few minutes of mumbling to herself, she threw herself against him, snuggling into his chest.

"I don't want to lose Tanya. I love being her teacher, but maybe I should ask the principal to transfer her out of my class," she said quietly. Rick nodded.

"I think it might be the best thing to do. I know you love your students, but her dad needs some correction."

"I'll talk to Dr. Manning tomorrow," Violet promised, referring to the principal, "Now can you please make love to me? I haven't seen my Lawman in four days, and I missed him."

"I missed you too, my Flower Girl," Rick whispered and leaned down to kiss her. Their lips met, and he felt the same rush of love and wonder he always did when he kissed this amazing woman. Violet moaned into his mouth, wrapped her tongue around his. Rick moved his hands down to cup her breasts, thumbing her nipples until they stiffened into peaks.

"Rick," Violet whispered his name, her voice filled with passion, "I want you so much."

"You got me, Flower Girl," Rick whispered back, "I'm right here, baby." He went back to kissing her, rubbing her soft breasts and tugging her nipples. Their mouths devoured one another, each of them desperate for the taste they'd been missing for nearly a week. Violet rubbed his chest, and moved lower, her hands splaying over his stomach and caressing him, like she was trying to re-familiarize herself. Rick pushed Violet onto her back, and moved over her, settling between her thighs. He began to kiss down her body, tasting her lips before sucking on her neck gently. He was careful not to leave a mark where her students could see. Violet writhed underneath him, rubbing his arms and spreading her legs wide. When Rick got to her breasts, he licked his lips. He sucked her nipples, one after the other, over and over, until Violet was shaking, and her nipples were hard and sensitive.

"Rick... baby, please," she begged. Rick laughed.

"Let me savor you, Flower," he told her, "I missed you, baby." He kept up his kisses and licks, teasing and tasting her nipples while she squirmed and begged underneath him. His hand moved from the curve of her hip to the juncture of her thighs and then he was playing in her pussy, coating his fingers with her arousal and making her cry out. Rick swiped her swollen clit with his thumb and Violet whimpered, coming in a flash, her eyes shut tight. He continued suckling at her, playing with her, doing to her body what only he could. When her breathing calmed, he pulled his hand and mouth away and moved downward, placing an open mouth kiss where his thumb had been seconds before.

"Fuck, Rick! Yes!" Violet cried, her hips bucking. She was unknowingly feeding herself to him, pushing her pussy against his warm mouth. Rick licked her cream, sucked on her swollen bud and kissed her pussy while she came for the second time, right over his waiting mouth.

As Violet tried to regroup, Rick moved up again, using his body to spread her thighs and then lifting them. He was inside her before she could speak, and her only response was a welcoming moan as she melted around him.

"Missed my Flower," Rick grunted, fucking her into the mattress, "Gimme my Flower." He moved with sure strokes, thrusting into her warm, wet home like he'd been gone for months instead of days. She was silky and tight around him, gripping him tautly, letting him know where he belonged. Rick agreed, and fucked her harder, determined to prove he was exactly where he wanted to be. Forever.

"Rick, oh shit—baby, I'm gonna—"

"You can, love," he urged her, feeling his balls tighten and his orgasm build, "I'm right here. I got you." They moved together, frantic in their lovemaking, their moans and low cries ringing in the otherwise quiet room. Rick leaned down, kissing Violet. They could be loud when they came together, and he didn't want to chance the noise waking Sasha. He felt the grip, the slight sting of Violet's nails in his back, and heard the scream she pushed into his mouth. Her pussy pulsed, grabbing him tight before attempting to push him out. Rick moaned and came, spraying her walls with his cum and falling onto her, wrenching his mouth away to take a deep, gasping breath.

He'd barely wiped Violet down before she was asleep and a minute later, he joined her, his mind clear and his body relaxed.

<u>*February 4th*</u>

"Baby Girl, what you want in your lunch?" Rick asked Sasha the next morning. Sasha finished her cereal and moved onto her banana.

"I want a Scooby Doo sandwich," she said, making him laugh. He'd introduced her to the cartoon and they both loved deli meat sandwiches, so she always called them that and loved getting them in her lunch. Rick quickly made her a honey turkey and cheese, wrapped her lettuce tomato, and pickles on the side, and gave her a bag of chips, a brownie bite, and some grapes. He finished with a juice box and a mini water bottle and handed her the lunch bag just as Violet came from the back, fully dressed.

"Y'all ready?" she asked, kissing Sasha on the forehead and him on the lips. Sasha nodded.

"Yeah. What you want for lunch? You can either have the dinner leftovers, or a tuna wrap and a thermos of soup," Rick said. Violet smiled at him, rubbing her hand over his.

"I'll take the leftovers. There's not enough for us to eat it again tonight anyway; might as well finish it off," she decided. Rick nodded and packed her lunch bag as well, and then they were all in his car, going to school. When he was with them, he always dropped them off and picked them up. His black F150 had automatic start so he was able to warm the car a little before they got in. Fifteen minutes later, they were at school, and he was kissing his girls goodbye.

"Get some rest, Lawman. Don't be at the house cleaning, and reorganizing, cause I know how you do. Your days off are days *off*," Violet told him.

Rick laughed. "I promise I'll nap and be lazy, Flower Girl. I'll be back to get y'all." She waved and took Sasha's hand, hurrying into the school.

Rick did nap for the rest of the morning, after he made and ate a huge omelet and bacon. He didn't feel like lunch, so he cleaned out his car and Violet's, sorted and started the laundry, then pulled out some chicken for dinner. Soon, it was time to pick his girls up, and Rick hurried to the school, wanting Tanya Richard's father to see him and feel his presence.

When he got to Violet's classroom, none of the kids had been picked up, so he sat in back, watching as parents, grandparents, nannies, and older siblings came one by one. At Violet's school, you couldn't wait outside for your parents until third grade.

"Hello again, Ms. Harrison," a voice said, and the contrived intimacy let Rick know this was Tanya's father. But the man didn't see him, so he played it cool.

"Mr. Richards. Come on, Tanya," Violet said, keeping it short. Tanya started packing her things. Mr. Richards placed his hands on the desk and leaned in. Violet shrank back.

"You give any thought to what I asked? We could be good," he asked. Rick was angry and sad. If he could hear him from the back of the room, he knew Tanya could.

Violet shook her head. "I'm involved, so are you, and I'm Tanya's teacher. Please stop."

"Why you play so hard to get?"

"She ain't playing," Rick said, speaking up and standing from his seat, "and neither am I." He walked to the front of the room, leaning in and lowering his voice, "I won't say what I want, because unlike you, I care that there's a child in the room. But hear me clearly: my woman said stop. And if you don't listen to her, I'm gonna see if you hear *me* next time. You got me?"

Tanya's father swallowed and nodded, his eyes wide with fear. Rick's presence surprised him.

"C-come on, Tanya," he called to his daughter, who was absorbed in her iPad. Tanya hopped up and ran to him, grabbing his hand.

"Please check your messages in the school portal when you get home. Principal Manning and I have made some changes," Violet said, turning away. Mr. Richards nodded again, taking his daughter and leaving. Rick leaned against the desk, still angry. Acting up in front of your children is never cool.

"You ready, babe?" he asked.

Violet nodded. "Yeah, Sasha's teacher usually meets me in the front hallway with her and we walk out together." She gathered her things, and Rick took her laptop bag and empty lunch bag. The classroom door opened again.

"Vi?" a man walked in, well-dressed but scruffy, rubbing his hands together. Violet dropped her handbag, looking like she'd seen a ghost.

"Alex? What are you doing here?" she whispered. The man stepped forward, smiling.

"I've come for you and Sasha. I've come for my family."

A Return Visit

February 4th
Violet Harrison

Violet Harrison couldn't speak. She couldn't breathe. What the hell was her ex doing here after all this time? He said he'd come for her, but she didn't even want to acknowledge the words. She refused to acknowledge the words. Rick was staring at her, his eyes questioning and angry. He wanted answers, and he deserved them. But Violet couldn't give him any until she got them for herself.

She shook her head, clearing it. "You what?" she asked her ex. He smiled.

Alexander Drake looked pretty much like she remembered—warm brown skin, hazel eyes, scruffy beard. He was bulkier than he'd been five years ago, and his hair was cut low instead of in straight backs, but he looked the same. The same playful gaze that stopped just short of telling the truth; the same hand-rubbing that made him look like a wolf staring at his prey; the same distrustful air, like there would always be something about him she didn't know. Violet shivered. She never felt like she had a handle on the situation when Alex was around. He'd always been a puppet master, pulling strings she couldn't see, trying to get her to do things she didn't want to do.

In contrast, Rick Wilkins was an open book, and nothing was sexier to Violet. From the way he'd honestly approached her, courted her, and told her everything about himself, she'd been swooning from day one. It didn't hurt that he was fine as hell too, with his copper-colored skin and deep, dark, smoldering eyes. He was fully bearded, with soft, juicy lips, a slightly narrow nose, and the longest lashes she'd ever seen on a man. Rick wore a simple low-cut Ceasar but kept his waves swimming and his line-up perfect. At thirty-nine, he looked like someone ten years younger, and he made Violet breathless every time he touched her.

Alex cleared his throat, getting her attention again, "I've come home, Vi. You and Sasha are my home, and I'm here to be with you."

"I'm sorry, but that isn't possible. I have—"

"A new man... and a new life. Rick Wilkins, and you are?" her lawman said, holding out his hand. Alex looked startled, as if he'd only just realized Rick was in the room. Violet smiled.

"Um... Alexander Drake. Sasha's father," he said, frowning a little, "How long has this been going on? You two?"

"Alex, you're not asking the questions here, I am. And you won't get any information until you answer them. What are you doing here?"

"I told you, Vi. I'm here for you. I'm here for Sasha," he insisted, smiling.

Violet shook her head. "You've been gone for five years. You can't just reappear like nothing happened, offering no explanation for where you've been, and trying to disrupt my life. I'm surprised you even remembered I work here. Nevertheless, your answer isn't good enough. Please leave." She picked up her handbag and reached for Rick's hand, pulling him toward the door before Alex got even more audacity and her lawman reacted.

"I want to see my child, Violet. I have a right to her!" Alex said, his voice raised. Rick let go of her hand and turned back. *Oh shit*, Violet thought.

"You have a right to whom? The child you abandoned when she was a year old. The child you threw away in a temper tantrum because Violet didn't want you. The child who doesn't even *know* you. You have a right to whom." Rick's voice boomed across the classroom and Alex took an involuntary step back. Violet grabbed Rick's arm.

"Not here, baby. Not where I work," she said to him, trying to keep Rick from losing his temper completely. Being a cop meant he was more conscious of losing control because of optics, but he was also a grown man who was very protective of her and Sasha and could only be pushed so far. Rick turned back to her, nodding his head. She held his hand tightly and took a deep breath.

"Alex, my life has moved on and so has Sasha's. She knows you exist, but she doesn't remember anything about you, and she hasn't asked. Our lives are happy, and you cannot show up here, with no warning, making demands when you've ignored her entire existence since you left. If you want to have an adult conversation about Sasha and the *possibility* of seeing her after you've proven yourself consistent, then let me know."

"Proven myself? I'm her father!"

"Who abandoned her and made no attempt to contact her. Even now, you're talking about coming home to your 'family'—as if a relationship with Sasha automatically means one with me. You can't even entertain fatherhood as a notion if it doesn't come with me attached. So *yes*—you will prove yourself before I think of allowing you near our daughter," Violet said, her anger rising. She'd worked hard to pick up the pieces after Alex let them fall, and she wouldn't be bullied by him after all this time. Rick stared down at

her, love and pride shining in his dark eyes. His smile was magnif-
icent, and Violet smiled back, immediately calmer.

"Oh, so Sasha's his daughter now? You got this nigga playing
Daddy?" Alex spat out, looking out of sorts and confused. At his
retort, Violet realized what she'd said, and why Rick looked at her
the way he had. She shrugged. There was no going back now. They
were a family. Rick leaned back toward Alex, a sinister smile on
his face.

"I'm not playing anything. Unlike you, I'm very serious about
my responsibility, which is why Sasha knows who I am. I've been
here, and I'll be here. You need to get used to it—because all roads
to *my* family, go through me," Rick growled and left the room,
pulling Violet behind him. Violet followed meekly, feeling a surge
of desire at the way her lawman commanded the room while con-
trolling his temper. He was everything, and she was going to climb
him like a tree for handling this so maturely. They got to the front
door, and Ms. Reynolds, one of the first-grade teachers, was there
with Sasha. As soon as her child saw them, she ran to Rick, and he
lifted her in his arms.

"We were about to come to your classroom and look for you,"
Ms. Reynolds said, smiling. Violet smiled back, relieved that they
hadn't.

"I'm sorry, girl. Got held up. Ladybug, tell Ms. Reynolds you'll
see her tomorrow."

"Bye, Ms. Reynolds!" Sasha waved, secure and happy with her
"Papa Rick." Violet vowed nothing would come between them, or
what she'd worked so hard for. Not even Alex.

February 6th
Violet

"Ms. Harrison, someone left a message for you here. He asked us to pass his number along so you can call him," Ms. Mahoney, the school secretary handed Violet a message slip as she entered the main office. Violet sighed. She knew it was Alex. After she and Rick left him in her classroom, it occurred to her he had no way of contacting her if he was serious about talking. She started to feel bad but changed her mind. She told herself he'd find a way if he really wanted to prove himself. It would seem he had.

"Thanks, Ms. Mahoney," she said and left the office. She hurried to the teacher's lounge to grab her lunch bag from the refrigerator. Lunch would be over soon, and she hadn't even had time to eat yet. Violet went to her classroom, sat down at her desk and unpacked her food. She'd told Rick to surprise her today, so she had no idea what it was, only that she needed to keep it cold. Violet pulled the container and opened the top, a smile splitting her face. Rick made her a packed chicken salad sandwich on the last brioche bun in the house. Brioche were his favorite, and she'd told him to use it for his breakfast sandwich. But as always, he made her smile instead. Eating the delicious sandwich, and drinking her juice was all she was able to do before the lunch aide brought the children back, so Violet cleaned up and focused for the rest of the afternoon. But the number Alex left sparked her curiosity.

"Do you want to call him?" Rick asked as she made dinner. It was a good time to talk since Sasha was napping, having fallen asleep in the car when they picked her up from dance class. Her loving lawman grocery shopped while she was at school, so she had nothing but options and decided to make his favorite seafood pasta, since he'd be going back to Luna Lake in the morning to start his four days on. Violet turned from the stove, staring into his eyes.

"Will it upset you if I do?" she asked sincerely. Rick smirked, shaking his head.

"Flower, I know you need to know why he did what he did, and how he plans to be different. I also don't want him to keep popping up and making you uncomfortable. Talking to him solves both of those things, so I'm okay with it. But you know... you could do it even if I wasn't."

"I know, baby. But I wouldn't. We're making a life, you and me. Your opinion matters to me, and I want to be transparent. Sasha and I love you and need you. I'm not letting Alex get in the way of our family, whether he's serious about a relationship with Sasha or not."

"Thank you, baby. I love you both, and I need you as well," Rick said, blowing her a kiss.

"Besides," Violet said, bending over to check the garlic bread she had in the oven, "did you not tell the man all roads go through you?" She grabbed her oven mitt to pull the sheet pan and set it on the stove. Rick was grinning when she turned to him again.

"I wasn't trying to be overbearing. I wanted to let him know he didn't need to come back playing that 'king of the castle' game. There's already a man sitting at the head of this table."

"And he's everything we need," Violet said, grinning back. "I think I'll call Alex, maybe meet up with him by myself first, and talk to him about offering financial support for Sasha. If he balks at it, I'll know where his head is."

"Good plan, Flower. If he expects to get the privileges of a relationship with her without having to take care of her, we'll know he's on some bullshit. But you know I'm back tomorrow. You want to wait until I'm off again? It doesn't take long to get here, but I'll still be in Luna Lake working if something happens."

"I will be fine, Lawman. If we meet, it will be in a public place, and I will carry my stun gun. Sasha's going to a sleepover so there's no chance of him seeing her and forcing the issue, and I will not be telling him where we live," Violet promised.

Rick nodded. "Text me his number and keep your location on."

"Yes, sir. Now please go get your daughter before she sleeps through dinner, and she's up all night," Violet shooed him out of the kitchen, and Rick headed to the back to wake Sasha.

February 8th

Violet sat alone at her favorite coffee shop, waiting for her ex to show up. After demolishing the seafood pasta and making love to her all night, her lawman left in the morning and was now on the second day of his 4/40. He'd called to wish her luck and remind her he loved her. Sasha was spending the weekend with her best friend Marnie—Marnie's parents were about the only ones she and Rick trusted, and the only place Sasha ever spent the night. Her daughter had assured her on video chat that she was "having the best time," which eased Violet's mind for this upcoming encounter with Alex.

Just as she was wondering if she should call Alex, he walked in, looking nonchalant, as if he were on time. He sat down, with a confused frown on his face.

"You didn't bring Sasha?" he asked. Violet stared at him, wondering if he was serious.

"No, I didn't. I told you we needed to establish some ground rules, and you'd have to prove your consistency," she told him.

Alex rolled his eyes. "Rules? What kind of rules?"

"We'll get to that. First, I want to know where you've been, Alex. What have you been doing? Why did you disappear, and why are you back?"

"I've been in Asheville—it's where I live now. I've been working and saving money. After you shut me out, Vi, I had to leave. What else was I supposed to do?"

"Alex, you're not answering the right question. I don't care why you left me. Why did you leave Sasha? You could have been a father without being my man," Violet said.

"I know, but I was hurt and acting out. I thought if I disappeared for a while, you'd realize how much you needed me. But then time passed, and you didn't ask me back. Before I knew it, a year had gone by, and I was embarrassed and ashamed, so I stayed away. I'm sorry, Vi. I am so sorry," Alex replied. His head was down, and his hands were clasped together.

"I see your companion has arrived. Can I get you folks something?" the server walked up to their table, all smiles and Violet nodded, feeling like this was a good time to take a breath.

"I'll have a large decaf mocha iced latte, and a croissant with strawberry jam. Alex?"

"Just a medium coffee, black," he mumbled. He reached across the table, and grabbed her hand. Violet almost wanted to pull away, but she didn't want to make a scene.

"I know I have a lot to make up for, Vi. All I'm asking for is a chance. You and Sasha mean everything to me," he said.

"Why are you back here now? I know something pushed you. Tell me what it is so I don't have to find out on my own," Violet said, instead of responding to his statement.

Alex sighed. "You're right, Vi. Truth is, I have another kid now—a son named AJ. He's three. His mother and I were never together; it was a one-night stand. We were getting along fine, coparenting, or whatever it's called, but a few months ago she met some guy and ran off. My mom came to help with AJ, and she started asking about Sasha and why I didn't have her too. I explained everything, and she said I needed to come here and make amends—get my family back. I realized she was right, and I came here to see y'all. But I really did miss you, Vi. I love you and Sasha, and I want to make it up to you, any way I can."

"You're here to be a father to my child, because you need a mother for *your* child?"

"No, it's not like th—Vi, listen to me—"

"Your mother doesn't want to help you raise your son, so she sent you to get me back so *I* can do it? Are you fucking serious, Alex?" Violet said angrily. The server came back, setting their drinks down and a small plate with Violet's pastry. Then she set down a ramekin with butter, and one with jam and smiled before walking away.

"Vi, I know how it sounds, but I really want my children to know each other. I really want to be the kind of father I should have been before. AJ's mom leaving showed me how hard you must have had it when I walked out. I need to make things up to y'all," Alex insisted.

"I appreciate you wanting to make things up to Sasha, but you don't need to make it up to me. And that's another thing we need to get clear. We fell apart, and then you didn't want to be Sasha's father because you couldn't be my man. *If* I decide to trust you with her, I need to know you can handle our situation this time. Because we're not going to be together—ever again. I love Rick, and I'm not moving backwards. Are you prepared to be our daughter's father without being with me, and accept Rick as a part of her life as well?" said Violet.

Alex scowled. "Why would Rick be a part of her life?"

"Because he's a part of mine. You're not listening!" Violet said, snatching her hand back. She took a deep breath, "Rick loves Sasha, and she loves him. He's been with us, and he takes care of us. At this point, he's known her longer than you. I'm not about to put him out of her life because you woke up and wanted to be a father after five years."

"Okay, Vi, okay," Alex grumbled, "I'll accept your little boyfriend."

Violet waved him off. "Please. He's my *man*, ain't nothing about him little, and you should be grateful he's accepting you. Now, we need to talk about some other things."

"What now?" Alex said, throwing up his hands. Violet sipped her latte, taking her time.

"Watch your tone with me. And since you asked, are you willing to contribute financially to Sasha's care and what kind of consistency will you have in seeing her? You live on the other side of the state."

Alex looked startled. "Contribute? How much? We'll have to work something out. I mean, I have AJ full-time, and his mom doesn't help."

"I have Sasha full-time, and *you* don't help," Violet pointed out.

"I thought you said your nigga was taking care of you?"

"Whether he does or not is irrelevant, because we're not talking about me. I'm asking you how you're going to help care for your child. You want to be in Sasha's life? A father provides."

"I really wasn't thinking about all that, Vi. I was hoping you'd let me bring my son down here so he could meet Sasha, and then we'd go from there," Alex shrugged.

"Go where? Because you don't live here. And you're most definitely not taking my baby home with you, so—you know what? I'm not doing this. Your mama sent you here with a half-ass plan to get me back and slide your son in so I could raise him too. You were hoping I was still single, and desperate enough to let you into my child's life even though you have no intention of taking care of her, and no plans on how to develop your relationship with her. You haven't asked a single question about Sasha since we sat down, and honestly, that should have told me something."

"You've been asking all the questions, Violet!" Alex yelled, getting angry.

Violet stood up. "And you haven't had any good answers. Call me when you get some." She dropped a ten-dollar bill on the table, left her coffee and her untouched pastry, and walked out. She got in her car and headed to Luna Lake. She needed to see her lawman.

Rick

"What's going on with you today?" Sabrina asked as they dropped Harlan Meadows off to his home again, "You've been distracted." Rick sighed. He couldn't get Violet and her ex out of his mind. She was meeting with him today, to discuss what role he expected to have in Sasha's life and how he'd earn it. He was worried about her, but more worried about the conversation. What was Alex saying to her? Was he spinning a perfect family fantasy for his Flower Girl? And was she falling for it?

"Violet's ex popped up a few days ago, says he wants his family back. Violet's meeting with him today," he finally admitted. Sabrina's eyes widened.

"Does she want him back too?"

"Of course not. Dude is a fucking bum. But Violet does think he deserves the chance to prove himself worthy of being a father, so she agreed to meet him."

"If she don't want him, why you look so worried?" Sabrina went on.

"Because as confident as I am, he's her child's father and he has nostalgia on his side."

"You think she'll fall for the okey doke? What you gonna do to change her mind?" Sabrina said, looking over him. Rick shrugged.

"I mean, what can I do at that point? I'm not gonna manipulate her into staying with me. I'm not him," he said. Sabrina laughed.

"Ain't nobody talking about nothing extreme. But this has to be a pain for her to deal with. Let her know you'll carry some of the burden. Remind her you ain't going nowhere, and she and Baby Girl are *your* family now. Stake your claim, man."

"All units be advised. We have a possible 10-40 at the Luna Lakeside Diner."

"A fight? At the diner? What the hell is going on? Tell them we're on the way," Rick instructed Sabrina as they drove away from their last call. Sabrina picked up the radio.

"Dispatch, this is unit 426, responding," she said, and turned on the siren. Two minutes later, they pulled up to the diner. A crowd of people were outside. Rick could see Hassan Meadows, Mr. Harlan's grandson and owner of *Luna Cutz*, the town's oldest barbershop. He was there with all his employees, some of the Hobbs clan, plus Ms. Minnie, the owner of the diner; Sassy Dumont, her most popular server, and what he guessed were patrons from inside, since some still had food in their hands. He and Sabrina got out of the car and headed for the fray, trying to break up the crowd.

"Alright, everybody back up!" Sabrina yelled, waving her baton and pushing people away. At the center of the crowd was Nate Harper, one of Hassan's barbers, and Sharif Sims, a barber at *Sharp Shears*, a popular barbershop chain whose location in Luna Lake was Hassan's biggest competitor. Rick inserted himself between the two men, dodging flying fists and pushing them apart.

"Enough!" he bellowed, and the two men backed off each other. Everyone quieted, and Rick pulled out his handcuffs.

"Who started this shit?" he asked. Sharif turned away, wiping his split lip and mumbling something under his breath. Nate straightened his clothes and then held his wrists out.

"He said something disrespectful to my... to Sassy, so I hit him. And if you and Bri disperse the crowd and he's still talking shit when you leave, I'm a do it again, so you might as well cuff me, Rick."

"Nathan, no! Rick, it wasn't his fault. It was a misunderstanding," Sassy said, coming to him with tears in her eyes. Sharif sneered at them, and Rick sighed, recognizing the jealousy right away. Nate looked at her.

"If you'd have let me handle it when I wanted to, he wouldn't have even thought he could say that shit to you, Syreeta. But it's cool. Come on, Rick. Let's get this shit over with. Hass, call my pops to post my bail," Nate spat out, cutting his eyes at Sassy. She cried harder and Ms. Minnie pulled her back into the diner. Sabrina was taking a statement from Sharif and Rick cuffed Nate, taking him to the cruiser and putting him in the backseat. After a couple of witness statements, Sabrina dispersed the crowd and everyone walked off, except Shakira Harlem, Sabrina's twin sister, who stayed to talk to her.

"No property damage and Sharif is headed to see if has a concussion, so we're good, Bri. What's up, Kira?" Rick said, walking up to them. Shakira hugged her sister and waved at him, heading back to Hassan's barbershop, where she worked. He and Sabrina got into the cruiser and pulled off.

Sabrina picked up the radio. "Dispatch, this is 426. We have one perpetrator in custody and we're all clear at the diner."

"*Copy that, 426,*" the dispatcher replied. Sabrina chuckled.

"Nathan, what the fuck were you thinking?" she asked. Rick glanced into the rearview mirror. Nate shrugged, his gaze focused on the passing streets.

"Wasn't my fault. Reef got all salty cause Syreeta moved on, and he said some out the way shit to her. I didn't let it slide."

"Then why were you so angry at Sassy?" Rick questioned.

"Cause her refusal to acknowledge us publicly might be reason he approached her in the first place. Syreeta is so fucking stubborn," Nate complained.

"She's a stubborn person you clearly love—you taking charges and shit," Sabrina laughed. Nate blew out his breath and shook his head. Rick felt sorry for him. It was obvious Sassy cared for him too but couldn't make it over the hump for whatever reason.

"Keep reminding her you ain't going nowhere," he said, repeating Sabrina's advice to him, "Sassy's scared. She needs to know you ain't gonna switch up or disappear. Take a break if you need one, but don't abandon her. If she's your heart, then stake your claim, man." Nate stared at him and then nodded his head. Rick pulled up to the police station and cut the engine. His cellphone buzzed on his hip.

"I got him," Sabrina said, "I'll see you inside." She got out of the car and opened the back door to get Nate out as Rick answered Violet's call.

"Hey, Flower Girl. I missed you."

A New Frontier

*F*ebruary 10th
　　Violet

Violet's bedroom was warm, and dark, passion and lust bouncing off the walls. The bed moved with the force of her and her sexy ass lawman's lovemaking, and she'd never been so hot and ready in her life.

After she'd gone to Rick in Luna Lake following her conversation with Alex, he took a break from work and comforted her with kisses and coffee. Violet admitted she'd always been afraid of Alex returning and expressed all her fears of Sasha's future reaction if she ever had to explain why Alex left, and why she turned him away when he returned. Rick was amazing, listening and prompting her to say what was on her mind. He told her he supported her and assured her she'd handled Alex the only way she could. Violet felt much better after seeing him and speaking to him. When she tried to apologize for coming to him while he was working, Rick scowled and told her to stop playing with him. Then he promised her he wasn't going anywhere and said as soon as he wrapped up his 4/40, he'd prove it. And here they were.

"Rickkkkk... shit, baby. I can't take it," Violet cried as she lay in her bed, getting fucked hard from behind. Her arch had slipped ages ago, and Rick was on top of her, his chest to her back, holding up one of her legs and using his hips to thrust into her again and again. He was so big, and so hard. Violet was nearly dizzy with pleasure, gripping the sheets and whimpering. She'd had to scream her first two orgasms into the pillows, so they didn't wake Sasha, and Rick showed no signs of slowing down. Her lawman was insatiable tonight, and she was blessed because of it.

"Yes, you can, Flower. Give me my flower. My soft, wet, sweet tasting flower. Give it to me," He talked her through it, his rumble in her ear only sending her further into the galaxy. He filled her, his dick stretching her so wonderfully. And she took him, gripped him tight, molded to him so perfectly she could only accept that her flower was indeed his.

"Baby, I'm coming," she wailed, and Rick chuckled, fucking her faster.

"Then come, Flower. Give me your sweet nectar. Leak for me," he whispered in her ear, and she obeyed him, her pussy contracting as she buried her face in the pillow and moaned his name. Her body felt like sparklers had exploded inside of her and she could barely see straight. Violet could hardly breathe, but she tried, gasping as she kept coming. Rick pulled out of her and turned her over, kissing her mouth. He spread her thighs and was back inside of her with one thrust, his powerful entry triggering aftershocks. Violet came again; she couldn't help it. She grabbed his biceps and closed her eyes, her back bowing.

"Ooooh shit," she whimpered, her body shaking. Rick started moving again, his forehead shiny with sweat. He lifted her legs over his arms and went deeper, making Violet cry out.

"Rick, you're so d-deep, baby. I-I can feel you—shit, fuck me. I c-can't—I can't—"

"I know baby," he whispered softly, looking into her eyes, "I know." His smooth, gentle voice was pushing her over the edge even faster. Violet was losing her mind while he calmly fucked her into oblivion, and she didn't know how she was supposed to go to school tomorrow and teach like nothing happened.

"Rick, I—"

"Come with me, Flower. Give me your sweet love, baby. Come with me," Rick said, pushing into her. Violet nodded, ready to travel to the clouds with him. Because with him asking so respect-fully, how could she refuse? The slap of their flesh meeting and the wet noises of Violet's pussy was the underscore to their moans and then it was happening. Rick pushed her legs back and buried him-self to the hilt, pumping until he released with a roar he muffled in her neck. Violet flowed wet around him, gripping his dick as she came too, her eyes rolling back from the sensations coursing through her body. Their mutual orgasm was one for the books, a reeling, continuous explosion that made them both call for each other. Then, they fell asleep.

"Mama. Mama. It's 7-3-0. We're supposed to wake up at 7-0-0," Sasha's insistent voice finally penetrated through the deep fog of sleep Violet was in. She opened her eyes, staring into the matching pair on the little person in front of her.

"What? Sasha are you okay, baby?" she croaked, trying to get her bearings. She was buried under a pile of blankets and her insa-tiable lawman, so it was slow going.

"Yes ma'am. It's 7-3-0," Sasha said again, and her words finally registered. Violet groaned.

"We're late. I'm sorry, Ladybug. Rick, we're late. Get up, baby," she said, pushing at her boyfriend, whose giant body was still cov-ering hers. He grunted and then lifted his head, opening his eyes.

"What?" he said. Violet smirked.

"It's 7:30," she told him, and turned back to her daughter as he shifted his weight off her, "Go wait for me in your room, Ladybug.

Mama will be right there." Sasha scurried off to do her bidding and Violet flopped back onto the pillows, laughing.

"I can't believe I let you fuck me unconscious, and I slept through my alarm."

"Take a mental health day. You and Baby Girl haven't had a day off since Christmas. We can lay around in pajamas and enjoy each other," Rick said, his gravelly, sleep-filled voice making her remember his passionate whispers from the night before.

Violet turned her head. "We should, huh?"

Rick grinned. "Hell yeah. Matter of fact, go head and call out and I'll wash up and get some pancakes started for Baby Girl." He got out of bed, stretching his muscled, but slightly pudgy, body. Rick worked out religiously, but he wasn't turning down a home-cooked meal or a cold beer. He went into the bathroom, blowing her a kiss when he caught her admiring his nakedness. Violet picked up her phone and dialed the school.

An hour later, all three of them were bathed and in pajamas, lingering over pancakes, sausage, and cheese eggs while they explained to Sasha what a "mental health day" was. Violet's phone buzzed and she picked it up, using her face to open it and read her texts.

Maybe Alex: I decided to go back home after our talk. I wasn't ready for what you needed from me, and I apologize. But I'll be back around for my girls. Both of them.

She snorted, shaking her head. He still didn't get it.

"What's wrong, babe?" Rick asked her. Violet shook her head and mouthed the word "Later" to him. She locked her phone.

"Nothing. Ladybug, you want to build your typewriter Papa Rick got you?" she asked and Sasha nodded, getting up from the table and running to her room. She expressed an interest in building things and so Rick had brought home a few beginners' *Lego* sets for her to try out.

Soon, they were in the living room, cuddled on the couch. Sasha was curled up on the loveseat; she'd settled into a nap after building her typewriter.

"Alex texted," Violet said, "He's gone back to Asheville. He apologized for not being what I needed and said he'd be back around for us one day."

Rick chuckled. "He's such a joke, man. I knew after you left him in the coffee shop, he'd be running home. He wasn't expecting to see you thriving; he was hoping you weren't so he could play on it."

"Nor was he expecting to see a real man here, filling in the gaps. He thought I'd be so desperate to give my child a father, I'd take anything, even him."

"Lucky for us, by the time he makes his way back, we'll be gone," Rick said. Violet looked at him quizzically. Were they going somewhere she didn't know about?

"What do you mean?" she asked. Rick stood up and got his bag from the entryway. He dug two folders out and brought them to her.

"I was worried when Alex popped up," he admitted, sitting down again, "I was worried nostalgia, and biology might win him some points with you. Then I realized I wouldn't have a reason to be worried, if I was staking my claim like a man should. You and Baby Girl are my family, and it's time I act like it."

"Rick, what are you—"

"I was saving this for Valentine's Day, but I'll be working the whole weekend anyway, and there's no more important day than the day a man proves himself to the woman he loves. I bought a house, on the west end of Luna Lake. It's close to the highway, so we can get to Wilmington easily. And it's close to the elementary school, whose principal happens to be looking for a second-grade teacher. There's a park a block away, and the house has a huge yard, with room for a playset, and a puppy for our girl."

"Oh, Rick—"

"I want you two to come be with me in Luna Lake. We're a family, and I can't ask you to share my life, when I'm keeping you separate from where it is. Come home, Flower. Come home to me. The house will be in both of our names as soon as you sign the papers, I have a ring whenever you're ready, and I'm gonna adopt Baby Girl—"

"I'm ready now," Violet interrupted, launching herself into his arms, "I'm ready now!"

"Hold on now. You gotta let me propose to you more romantically than that," Rick said, kissing her softly, "But will you and Sasha move into our new home with me?"

Violet nodded her head, her throat clogged with tears. This lawman of hers had outdone himself, and she was overwhelmed in the best way. He'd bought a house for them, found a job for her, and made sure things were in place for Sasha. Though the distance was short, not being with him every night was starting to wear on her, and on Sasha. They missed him terribly, but Violet was always hesitant to complain. He took such good care of them, and it made her heart thump to know he'd wanted them all together just as much.

"Yes, Rick," she said, tears falling, "we'd love to come and live with you. We love you so much."

"I'd like to ask Sasha when she wakes up, make sure she knows I care about her opinion as well. Would you be okay with us asking her together?" Rick said, and Violet's heart beat even faster. How was this man every damn thing?

"Yes, of course, but the playset and the puppy are going to seal it for her, just so you know," she said, laughing. Rick kissed her, wrapping her in his arms and pulling her close. Violet moaned softly, kissing him back, melting into his embrace.

February 14th
Rick

Rick was in a bad mood. He and Sabrina had been driving around town all day, dealing with call after call. He didn't understand so much animosity on the day of love. Plus, he'd had to leave his woman and child that morning, so he was extra grumpy.

"You got any plans after shift?" Sabrina asked him as they parked to enjoy the coffee they'd picked up from the drive-through. Luna had a total of six fast food restaurants, and they did well, but they were still no match for Lakeside Diner, Maddy's Ice Cream Shop, BJ's Soul Food, Fresh Catch Seafood Palace, or any of the other local eateries. Luna Lake folks were loyal to their small businesses. Rick shrugged.

"My girls aren't here, and going to them when I have to be right back on shift at 6am seems pointless, you know? I want to be able to enjoy them. Violet sent some leftovers back with me; I'll probably eat them and watch basketball in my recliner until I fall asleep."

"Boring! Did you at least send Violet some flowers?"

"I sent a huge bouquet to the school, with some chocolate and a bear for Violet and a mini version of everything for Sasha," Rick said. Violet and Sasha called him on video chat at lunch, both smiling so wide his heart thumped.

"Awww, I love this for you! Rick Wilkins, becoming a family man, for real!" Sabrina said.

"And thinking about switching it up even more," he went on.

"How so?"

"The state gave the police department additional funds and a grant to add a couple of crime prevention positions—youth advocates, criminal researchers, law and policy analysts. I'm going to apply for one of them."

"Wow Rick," Sabrina said, "You're really making big changes."

"I have to. Being a cop, even in a relatively quiet place like this one, wears on you after a while. Plus, nowadays it represents something I'm not sure I want to anymore, you know?"

"I do know, and I get it. Congratulations, man."

"Thanks, Bri. What about you? You got plans tonight?" Rick asked his partner.

Sabrina groaned. "My sister and her boo are going to BJs for dinner, and they're bringing his single cousin, so I'm meeting them there for the set-up."

Rick laughed. "It might be nice, Bri. He could be a good dude."

"I guess," she scowled, "But me being a cop usually intimidates them, and my sister always makes me sound like a dating charity case with cobwebs on her cooch. I don't want him to think I'm desperate, but knowing Kira, he already does."

"Let me guess: then you act distant, to overcompensate for what she's told them, and end up looking standoffish and stuck-up"

"Exactly! But I promised I'd give this one a chance, so I'm going."

"*All units be advised. We have a 10-56 at the Luna Lake Community Center.*"

"Gotdammit, Mr. Harlan," Rick grumbled. 10-56 was the code for public disturbance or intoxication, "Tell them we're on the way."

Sabrina giggled. "Dispatch, this is 426, responding."

Thirty minutes later, Mr. Harlan was home, and Rick was ready to wrap up this shift. They had a couple more minor calls—noise complaints from the neighbors of folks who were already celebrating Valentine's Day—but it was mostly quiet. When Rick and Sabrina finally got off patrol at 4pm, and separated after finishing paperwork, Rick had never been so happy to head home. When he got home, Violet's car was in his driveway, and he got worried. Had Alex shown up again? He pulled in behind her and got out of his truck, his shoulders drooping. He was tired, and he needed a shower, but also, he was anxious to get inside and see Violet.

"Hey, Officer Wilkins!" Jade yelled his name from her stoop, and he threw up a half-hearted wave, anxious to get into the house.

"You eat yet? Got some smothered pork chops ready!" she continued. Before Rick could open his mouth to refuse her—yet again—his front door opened.

"My lawman don't need you to feed him, Ms. Girl. How many times he got to tell you he don't want your food, or anything else you got?" Violet said, stepping onto the porch. Rick stopped, amused.

Jade sputtered, her light face reddening with embarrassment. "I don't—I didn't know—"

"This man is *mine*; you hear me? And I got him. Officer Wilkins is very well taken care of, thank you. Go bang them pots for somebody else. Smell like you scorched the damn gravy anyway," Violet said, hands on her hips and a scowl on her face. Jade gasped and rushed back inside, slamming her door. Rick stared at his girlfriend, and then doubled over in laughter.

"Flower Girl, why you do her like that?" he asked, laughing as he slammed the truck door, hit the key fob and hurried to the front steps. A moment later, he had Violet in his arms, her whiskey eyes filled with annoyance, and her soft mouth in an adorable pout. He kissed her lips until she relaxed them and moaned into his mouth.

"How many times I gotta tell somebody to leave my man alone? Good thing we're moving," she said. Rick laughed again, squeezing her. He was so happy to see her.

"What are you doing here?" he asked. Violet grinned and stepped back, pulling him inside. His living room was decorated with pink and red balloons. The flowers he'd gotten both Violet and Sasha decorated his coffee table, and his baby girl was sitting on the floor, cutting hearts out of construction paper.

"Papa Rick!" she yelled, when she looked up and saw him. Rick scooped her into his arms and hugged her.

"Hey, Baby Girl. What are you doing here?"

"Me and Mama surprised you for Valemtime's Day," she announced, a huge smile on her face.

"I see. I am sure surprised. And so happy to see you both," he said. He set Sasha down and came further into the house, "It looks great in here. Thank you. I really missed y'all."

"We missed you, Papa Rick. Mama made your favorite, and we have brownies in the oven, too," Sasha chattered.

"You do? Wow. This is the best day ever, then," Rick grinned.

"Come on, Ladybug. Let your dad get out of his uniform and take a shower. We'll check on the brownies," Violet said and took Sasha's hand. They went into the kitchen, while Rick stood there, stuck, a goofy grin on his face. They came because they were anxious to be with him. And Violet had called him Sasha's dad.

After a perfect dinner of Marry Me Chicken over mashed potatoes and a Ceasar salad, the three of them shared a huge brownie sundae while they watched TV.

"Okay, Ladybug, remember our agreement?" said Violet. Sasha stood up, nodding her head.

"Yes, ma'am. I'll go get ready for my bath," she said, and ran off to the second bedroom, which was essentially his office, but he'd added a daybed for Sasha.

Rick turned to Violet. "What agreement?"

"We both decided we missed you and wanted to come see you, but I told her that if we came and interrupted your night, she couldn't make a fuss at bedtime, because you have to work and you're going to bed early too."

"Bite your tongue, woman," Rick chastised, nuzzling his girl-friend's neck, "My girls are not an interruption, and you can both be wherever I am, at any time. Also, y'all don't have to go to bed because I'm going. My home is yours, and it's the weekend. Fall asleep on the couch watching movies. I don't care."

Violet shook her head. "When you come to us, you're off work, but you still operate on our schedule, even though you don't have to. We're going to do the same. Now, you get into your pajamas and wait for me. I'm gonna give this girl a quick bath and meet you in our room."

Rick nodded and Violet gave him a quick kiss before getting up. Rick locked everything down, started the dishwasher, and went into his room, doing a quick wipe down and face scrub since he'd showered before dinner. He sat on the bed in his T-shirt and boxer briefs, doing some stretches. He heard his girls laughing together, and water splashing. Rick waited ten minutes, then put on his robe and went next door. Violet was tucking Sasha into the daybed, whispering to her while she giggled.

"Came for story time and to say goodnight, Baby Girl," he said, sitting next to the bed. He kissed Sasha on her forehead and held her hand. Sasha yawned and smiled at him. Violet started reading, her voice soothing and gentle. She didn't get halfway through the book before Sasha's lids were drooping.

"Goodnight, Sasha," Rick crooned.

"Goodnight, Daddy," the little girl whispered, and her eyes shut. Rick was speechless, sitting on the floor, staring at Sasha like she might disappear. His eyes filled with tears. Violet turned to him, not even hiding hers. He stood up, kissing Sasha's forehead one more time and pulling Violet from the room. They pulled the door to, but not closed and went next door. The two of them sat on the edge of the bed, leaning against each other.

"She called me—"

"It's who you are to her, Rick. It's who you've been from the beginning," Violet said. A few more minutes passed, and Violet kissed his cheek and went to shower. Rick sat there with his thoughts. He had the family he dreamed of, and things were falling into place the way he always hoped. He vowed to hold his family close, stake his claim, and never let anyone take them away.

"Happy Valentine's Day to me," he whispered, chuckling after. Rick was in bed when Violet slid in beside him, immediately snuggling close. He gathered her in his arms.

"Hold me, Lawman," she demanded, wrapping herself around him, "hold me so tight."

"I'll hold you forever, Flower Girl."

Books Mentioned

SINFUL DESIRE BY ASIA MONIQUE

I WANNA BE DOWN BY ASHLEY NICOLE

WE'VE ONLY JUST BEGUN BY NICOLE FALLS

BEING MERRY BY MEKA JAMES

BEING HOSPITABLE BY MEKA JAMES

SEEING RED BY SHON

Acknowledgements

Jaleesa Jackson - Always, and in all ways. Love you.

Kimmie Ferrell- Thank you for always encouraging me, for knowing Luna Lake was still in me, and for reminding me they needed a new band director. Love you.

Solidarity and Kahree Taylor- As the unpartnered member of the crew (lol), y'all have been the soul mates I needed, and the examples of romantic love I want to follow.

Torri Reed- When did you become the voice in my head? Lol. Probably right around the time you started answering my voice notes. Love you.

Nina High, Ayla Cox, Lesanda Moore, Treasure Malian, Sky Nova, Coya Wilson, Jessica Terry, Turtleberry, Lily Flowers, Ciana Smoak, Olivia Linden, Ke'Asia Morris, and Pamesh--Thanks for letting me collab with you, and helping me boost my work.

About the Author

Shameka Erby is a writer from Philadelphia currently living in Baltimore.

Her love affair with romance novels started early, and she loves writing sweet and sexy love stories. Now the author of both short story collections and many romantic novels, Shameka's joy is in writing gentle, emotional, passionately heated stories of Black love starring plus sized and queer characters. She also publishes a newsletter, *Just A Girl and Her Laptop*.

Books By Shameka S. Erby

The McNeal Love Stories
The Drivers Seat
Find My Way Back
The Officer and the Butterfly
The Greatest Risk

The Royals
Hooked on Your Love
Until You Come Back To Me
All I Need
Don't Play That Song
The Going Away Present: A Mal & Luchi Short
Love Notes: Sexy Holiday Stories

Coming Home: The Elements Series
The Air Between Us
Her Solid Ground
His Fire & His Ice
The Pick-Up

Luna Lake
All I Want For Christmas Is Two
Hearts Afire: Love in Luna Lake
The Fire We Make
Double Trouble: Christmas in Luna Lake

www.ingramcontent.com/pod-product-compliance
Lightning Source LLC
Chambersburg PA
CBHW071744150726
47998CB00005B/1800